Frank Barrett

Little Lady Linton

A Novel: Vol.III.

Frank Barrett

Little Lady Linton
A Novel: Vol.III.

ISBN/EAN: 9783337031596

Printed in Europe, USA, Canada, Australia, Japan

Cover: Foto ©Andreas Hilbeck / pixelio.de

More available books at **www.hansebooks.com**

A Novel.

BY

FRANK BARRETT,

AUTHOR OF 'FOLLY MORRISON,' 'HONEST DAVIE,' ETC.

IN THREE VOLUMES.

VOL. III.

LONDON:

RICHARD BENTLEY AND SON,

Publishers in Ordinary to Her Majesty the Queen.

1884.

CONTENTS OF VOL. III.

iv   *Contents.*

LITTLE LADY LINTON.

CHAPTER I.

NARRATIVE.—LITTLE LADY LINTON RECEIVES
AN OLD FRIEND OF HER HUSBAND'S.

ITTLE LADY LINTON sat in
the salon of her home at
Valvins. Her dream of happiness was realized.

The windows of the low front abutting
upon the lawn were thrown wide open, and
the soft morning breeze came in sweet with

the fragrance of the jessamine that overran
the veranda. There was just enough wind
to set the river sparkling, and to make the
tall aspens bend and cause a cheerful
rustling among their leaves. The atmo-
sphere was bright and fresh; the flower-
beds that bordered the lawn were gay with
colour. In the paddock beyond, the grass
had been allowed to stand and run to seed ;
it came up to the knees of the dun cow,
and Gertie could only see the back of the
old goat as she steadily browsed, and the
heads of her young as they frisked and
leapt. Everything was pleasant to the
senses and exhilarating.

Gertie was alone, stitching; a dainty little
work - table stood between her and the
veranda, so that when she paused in her
work to get a fresh length of cotton, she
could look out over her garden and paddock

and see the silver river between the tall poplars on the right.

That is just what she was doing when her ear caught the sound of a voice humming a tune. In a moment she slipped her work into the well of the little table, closed the top, and, folding her arms upon it, leant forward with her head a little on one side, and ooked out in the direction from which the sound had come, her eyes prettily twinkling with pleasure and her cheeks just tinged with a blush.

Gilbert strolled over the lawn with a garden-basket in his hand, and came towards the house. The morning sun was in his eyes when he looked towards the salon, and he failed to see Gertie. Still humming, he paused under the veranda and picked a spray of jessamine; then, having laid it in the basket, he was about to stroll off towards the terrace, when a little pearly laugh told him that the object of his search was close at hand and observing him.

'You there, Gertie?' he said, turning back.

He came into the room, taking off his soft felt hat, and laid the spray on the table. Gertie leant back in her chair and stretched her arms upwards in silence, looking into his face with a beseeching love in her eyes and lips. He stood over her for a moment, then bent down, and she clasped her hands upon his neck and held him prisoner. When he was released, he drew a chair near her and seated himself.

'Found half a dozen apricots — ripe,' he said, putting the basket in her lap. 'I intended them as a bribe; but somehow they don't seem quite adequate to the purpose now.'

'What purpose?'

'Thought I might tempt you to go out.'

'I can't walk far, dear,' she said, her cheek and neck flushing with a deeper pink.

'No necessity. Sit in the boat, and I'll row you—lounge in the chaise, and I'll drive you. It's a heavenly morning.'

'So it is, love.' She took the basket from her lap, as if to rise. 'Where shall we go?'

'What does that matter to you?' he asked, after looking at her for a moment, in silent devotion. 'If I asked you to go to the North Pole you'd consent, and think it the pleasantest promenade in the world. Sit down, Gertie; there's no hurry. It's as pleasant here as elsewhere, perhaps.'

He threw his arm over the back of the chair and talked of trifles—of matters concerning the garden and the stable and their projects for the summer ; and she gave herself up to the pleasure of an idle chat, eating now and then from the fruit in the basket he had brought her, laughing lightly at his jokes, and thinking that surely no one on earth could talk so charmingly as he, who found without effort something pleasant to say upon whatever subject he talked, and paid her a hundred graceful compliments without seeming to seek for one. She had thought him perfect in the old time, when often his manner was cynical and hard ; but, ah, he was far more lovable now that his bearing was gentler and more sweet. And the change was more delightful to her, because it arose from his greater happiness.

They gossiped for half an hour, and then,

changing his position, he perceived a reel of cotton at his feet. He picked it up carelessly, and was about to lift the top of the work-table, when she, with a little cry of alarm, put her hands upon it and held it down.

' Ah,' he said, with a little look of surprise, ' you, too, Gertie, have a secret!'

She nodded—smiling and blushing at the same time.

' Thank God, it's a happy one,' he said, rising and looking down at her with tender earnestness. ' I see now why you did not want to go out.'

' I did not say I wished to stay at home.'

' I found that out for myself. I shall ride over to Marlotte; that will give you three or four hours to gloat over your secret.'

He stooped down to kiss her.

'Aren't you jealous?' she asked, holding his head between her hands and looking into his eyes.

'Not a bit.'

'And aren't you burning with curiosity to know what it is you mustn't see?'

'Men are superior to that sort of feeling, you know.'

Gertie still held him, and seemed to be rather disappointed at his lack of interest.

'Wouldn't you like to see just a tiny morsel of it?' she asked.

'Come to look at it in that light, I think I should.'

In joyful haste, tempered with elaborate caution, she opened the work-table a few inches, peeped in, then drew out about four inches of a marvellous little cambric sleeve.

'Good heavens, Gertie!' said he, after regarding it in perplexity for a moment, as he sank into his chair, ' you don't mean to hint that you still go in for dolls!'

' Dolls!' she exclaimed, with an accent of supreme disgust.

More perplexed than ever, Gilbert looked from his wife to the little sleeve, touched it, and lifted his eyes again to Gertie's flushed face; then, as a ray of intelligence flashed upon his mind, he dropped the sleeve which he held between his thumb and finger, and, leaning forward, took her hand, and said under his breath :

' Is my little wife to be a mother?'

She snatched her hand from his, flung her arms round his neck, and pressed her burning cheek to his for reply.

Gilbert had been gone an hour. Gertie's radiant face was bent over the work; her nimble fingers drew the thread with such care as the most delicate embroidery might require. The door behind her opened, and Mrs. Pierce entered the room and approached her mistress with the noiseless step and restrained bearing of a well-trained servant.

Mrs. Pierce was a slight wiry woman of about forty years, dressed in a plain black gown and rigid cuffs and collars, and a white apron and cap. Her appearance was particularly neat; she looked, no matter when, as if she had just come from making her toilette. Her hair seemed to be cemented to her head; her complexion was dark, her nose straight and sharp, her upper lip long and divided from the lower by the straight and faintly perceptible line of her mouth. Every movement was painfully precise; only her little stone-grey eyes seemed capable of precipitate and irregular motion.

'Will her ladyship be good enough to instruct me with regard to the dinner?' she asked, adopting the correct manner of French servants.

Gertie laid her work in her lap and discussed the subject at some length, choosing this dish and rejecting that, as she considered her husband's taste ; occasionally Mrs. Pierce made a respectful suggestion, which was invariably good. The admirable servant seemed to know her master's tastes as well as Gertie herself, and her excellent memory furnished her with abundant alternatives. If one thing was not to be had, another would serve as well. She opposed nothing, but contrived to make everything possible. While the question was yet under consideration, the visitors' bell rang. Gertie received so few visits that the sound of the bell was a matter of importance to her. Instinctively she raised the top of her work-table to put away her work, half rising from her chair. Mrs. Pierce shot a glance through the window as far as her eye could reach in the direction of the visitors' entrance, and back again to her mistress ; otherwise she did not move a muscle.

'That was the visitors' bell, Pierce.'

' Yes, madam. Would her ladyship like me to ascertain who has called?'

' Yes, by all means. Philippe of course knows what to do ; but you can bring me the card.'

Mrs. Pierce left the room, and Gertie began to pick off some threads of cambric that clung to her dress, in case she had to see the visitor. Possibly it was M. de .Clameran, or some other friend of her husband's. It seemed a long time between Pierce's going and her return. At length she came into the room, closed the door behind her, crossed with her customary precision to where Gertie stood, and said :

'The lady has not a card——'

'Lady ! Is it a visitor for me, then ?'

'No, madam. The lady desired to see Sir Gilbert. Her name is Miss Drummond.'

'She is English !'

'Yes, madam. I told Miss Drummond that Sir Gilbert was absent, and that I would inform you of her presence. She is in the morning-room.'

'That will do, Pierce. I will see the lady at once. I think we have settled about dinner.'

'Yes, madam.'

Pierce crossed the room and opened the door ; and Gertie passed out, wondering who this visitor was whose name she had never heard her husband mention. She crossed the vestibule and, with a timid hand—she was nervous, she knew not why—opened the door of the morning-room. She entered the room so noiselessly that the sound did not disturb Miss Drummond, who, standing in the middle of the room, with her back to the door, was evidently examining the luxurious apartment critically. Gertie stood still for a moment, only just able to form some idea of the visitor from that point of view. Except that she was taller and broader than most Frenchwomen, the visitor looked more like a Parisian than an Englishwoman. There was something strongly suggestive of the Boulevard des Italiens in her hat, with its over-abundant garniture of feathers and fruit, in the elaborately ornamented mantle that nipped her elbows into her waist, in the stiff silk skirt trained out behind, with its border of white balayeuse. Gertie dared hardly whisper to herself, as she closed the door, that her husband's acquaintance seemed rather showy than ladylike.

Miss Drummond heard the door shut, and turned round at once, with a kick at her train.

Gertie loved the fashions as well as any woman, and to her one of the chief attractions of Paris was its parade of richly dressed women. Yet the pleasure she found in looking at them she lacked in regarding Miss Drummond, and this notwithstanding that she was considerably better-looking than the generality of Frenchwomen, and that nothing could have been richer or more costly than the dress she wore. The thing which spoilt all was the expression in Miss Drummond's face, and something in her manner which was

not ladylike.   She was like an actress who,
over-acting her part, destroys the illusion
she would create. Miss Drummond's hair,
dressed in the latest style of Sarah Bern-
hardt, was a little too golden, her lips too
red, her skin too fair, her eyebrows too
dark, and an air, intended to be haughty,
being overdone, became simply impudent,
an effect heightened by a pair of pince-nez,
which, worn rather low on her nose, compelled her to throw her head back before
she could fairly see Lady Linton.

She stepped forward to meet Gertie,
swaying her rustling skirts from side to
side, and with one hand extended as far
as the mantle which confined her arm
allowed.

'My dear Lady Linton,' she said, making
two syllables of the word 'dear,' 'so happy
to know you—so very happy !'

Gertie replied in formal terms, wondering where it was she had previously heard the letter 'h' aspirated with such intensity.

'What a charming spot you have chosen to live in, and what an elegant little house !'

Again Gertie replied with a stock phrase. She remembered now that the young lady at the milliner's in Regent Street, where Gilbert had taken her, aspirated her 'h's' and cut her diphthongs in half.

'And how is dear old Bertie ?' asked Miss Drummond.

'Bertie !' echoed little Lady Linton, in amaze.

'Pardon me. I suppose I ought to call him Gilbert now. We were old sweethearts, you know.'

'Indeed I don't know. My husband has

never, to my knowledge, mentioned your name to me.'

'Oh, the odious monster! I will punish him for this. He shall not have a moment's peace until he has apologized to both of us.'

'My husband apologizes to no one.'

'Not when he does wrong?'

'He never does wrong.'

'Oh, you dear charming little innocent! Don't you see that in this very matter he has wronged you most horridly? I am not seeking a compliment, you know.'

If she had been, she was not likely to get one from Gertie at that moment.

'No,' she said; 'I see nothing of the kind.'

'He has wronged you by treating you as a child, and supposing you would be jealous and hurt to find that he wasn't immaculate.

Oh, these men ! They think that every woman they love is a fool, to be cheated by their professions or deceived by their silence. As if we didn't know what they do behind our backs, and were blind to the facts that stare us in the face ! Perhaps it's as well, my dear, to let them go on thinking we are fools, or they might cease to love us.'

Miss Drummond had seated herself in a causeuse, and spoke with her head leaning on the back, swinging her foot to and fro carelessly as she stared with half-closed eyes at Gertie. Gertie sat and listened in a state of bewilderment, with a feeling of anger gnawing at her heart. What was she to do ? How was she to reply ? She felt as though she had been suddenly transported out of her own world into one where the customs and language had all to be learnt before she could understand her position. Miss Drummond seemed to her like the vulgar woman in that book of Ouida's which she had read ; but perhaps she was a fair specimen of the class to which Gilbert belonged, and in which she must take her place. She remembered that Ouida's most vulgar and unpleasant women were represented as being superior to middle-class people. Perhaps Miss Drummond was only indulging in a kind of persiflage that did not represent her real feelings. One thing was certain ; she must repress her anger, whether it was well or ill founded, and receive her husband's friend with becoming civility.

'I do not expect Gilbert to return for some hours,' she said, with a little twitch-ing at the corner of her lips, which was the nearest approach to a smile she could assume. ' You will stay to dinner ?'

'Thanks—very much, thanks. I came with the intention of staying if I found you agreeable. It would be a very poor compliment if I didn't carry out my intention now I have told you that.'

'You are very kind,' murmured poor little Lady Linton, her heart failing at the prospect. 'Is your carriage coming?'

'There are two or three boxes and my dressing-case at the hotel at Fontainebleau —Hôtel d'Angleterre. If you will send one of your people for them, so that I may have a decent dress for dinner—I know how particular Bertie is—it is right he should be, for I consider nothing more despicable than an ill-dressed woman, except an ill-dressed man. Men have no excuse. I should consider it an insult if a man sat down at table with me in anything but evening-dress.'

'Gilbert finds evening-dress comfortable, otherwise I don't think he would wear it. He dines in his shooting-jacket when he feels indisposed to trouble himself with dressing or is tired with walking.'

'I would allow no excuse, my dear. Men presume upon privileges of that kind, and dislike you for permitting them. Why do ninety-nine men out of a hundred prefer the society of any woman to their wives? Simply because the wives are foolish enough to permit a certain degree of familiarity which nauseates them. I admit, however, that leniency was the fault of your predecessor.'

' My predecessor ?'

' Bertie's first wife, my dear.'

' Ah, you knew Lady Linton ?'

They were in the bedroom now; and Miss Drummond, standing at the toilet-table, was trying one after the other of the scent-flacons. She inhaled a long whiff of eau-de-Cologne, and replied :

'Yes, I knew her very well.'

'You visited at the Abbey ?'

Miss Drummond, still smelling the bottle, closed her eyes and inclined her head, her lips a little parted, drawn back, and showing a line of white teeth.

'Awfully nice time there !' she observed, scarcely moving her lips from the unpleasantly straight line in which they were contracted upon her teeth.

Gertie wondered if it was at the Abbey, and during his wife's lifetime, that Miss Drummond and Gilbert had been sweethearts ; and, with a feeling akin to shame, she recalled the love-passage which had taken place between herself and him in Monkden woods.

'Bertie was horribly bothered there; but it improved him. Men with bad wives are always interesting. They feel it necessary to be on their best behaviour with other women, you know. There's a certain fascination about them that's irresistible. Haven't you found it so, dear?'

She had seated herself with the flacon, and, still inhaling the perfume, looked at Gertie.

'I have had very little experience,' stammered Gertie, turning red and white. 'Perhaps that is why I find the subject not a very pleasant one.'

'Do you really wish me to believe that the subject is unpleasant to you?'

'Undoubtedly. I assure you it is.'

'Excuse me if I find it difficult to believe. My observation has led me to believe that it is the only subject that has any interest to women ; all others are more or less agreeable as they bear upon that one theme of the relation between men and women.'

Gertie made some commonplace rejoinder, and then, anxious to escape, changed the subject, and left the room to despatch a cart to Fontainebleau for Miss Drummond's baggage. That done, she went into the salon and sat down, with her hands in her lap, to think it all over and so arrange her ideas that she might be able to get through the day without making a fool of herself and giving Gilbert cause to regret her want of worldly wisdom. She heard the tinkle of a bell, and shortly afterwards Pierce came into the room, with her noiseless step and rigid composure.

'If you please, your ladyship, Miss Drummond desires some sherry.'

CHAPTER II.

SIR GILBERT ENCOUNTERS MISS DRUMMOND.

IT was five o'clock when Gilbert returned from Marlotte. As he passed the terrace he caught a glimpse, through the shrubbery, of a light costume under the veranda, and raised his hat. He rode in by the stable-entrance, threw himself off his horse, and went round by the lawn. A little way from the window he met his wife.

' Why, Gertie, what is the matter ?' were his first words, as he took her hands in his and looked in her face with anxious questioning.

A few hours since he had left her radiant with happiness ; he found her now with an expression of fatigue and constraint in her face, as though she had endured some acute physical suffering and wished to conceal it from him.

'Nothing, dearest,' she answered faintly ; and then, after a hasty glance behind her, as if to assure herself that she was not observed, she nestled her face against his breast to conceal her ill-disguised emotion.

He felt her body trembling under his hands, and led her away to a seat in the shadow of the house.

'Come, what is it, love ?' he asked, drawing her close to him when they were seated.

'Oh, I'm a goose—that's all, dear!' she murmured, trying to laugh. 'We mustn't sit here. Go into the library, please; there's a surprise for you.'

'Not an agreeable one, I should say, by the look of things,' he said. 'It's a sufficient surprise to find you so changed since we parted. I don't want another of the same kind. Let me know what I am to expect.'

'Your cousin has come to see us.'

'My cousin!' he exclaimed slowly, in a tone of wonder.

'Miss Drummond. She arranged it all. I didn't think you would care very much to be surprised in that way. But, as she said it would be a pleasant surprise for you, and as she is your cousin, you know, dear, and our visitor, I couldn't object.'

'My cousin—Miss Drummond!' Gilbert

repeated, in a voice which was scarcely audible.

'She was stopping at an hotel at Fontainebleau, on her way to Monaco; and, hearing there that we lived so close, she thought it would be—be—"awfully nice," she said, to come and stay with us for a few weeks.'

Gilbert said nothing, but the arm that surrounded his wife's waist twitched convulsively.

'Of course, dearest, I am very pleased indeed that your cousin—that anyone you like should come to see you and stay with us,' Gertie said earnestly. 'I am only troubled because I begin to see how far removed I am from the class of society to which you belong—because I see how childish and silly I must look beside women who know the world better than I do—because I can't converse about the ordinary topics of good society, or even understand them, and so must sit silent and stupid-looking when I ought to be entertaining and bright.'

Gilbert said not a word to encourage his wife; he only drew her a little closer to him.

Gertie was glad he did not speak; it gave her an opportunity to say all that she had on her mind. The presence of his loving arm gave her confidence in his sympathy and tolerance.

'You see, dear,' she pursued, 'I have never known any grand people, except you; and you are so different to all the world.' She broke off to lift her face and kiss his beard. 'I have mixed only with very simple people, the peasants at Neufbourg, and Mrs. Simpson at Kennington, and I

have naturally fallen into their way of looking at things ; and now, being brought
suddenly into the society of such a lady
as your cousin, and having to remodel
everything in my mind, I feel as if a long
lesson were set before me to master all at
once.'

'Where is she?' asked Gilbert, when
Gertie ceased to speak.

'In the library, dear.' His left hand
was in her lap—she lifted it gently to
her lips.

He seemed not to notice it.

'I am glad to tell you this, dear,' she
went on, stroking his hand tenderly—' not
that I think you would misunderstand me
if I hadn't told you. You love me so that
you would never doubt my wish to be
pleasant to your friends, however stupid
and dull I might seem, would you ?'

' Oh, that's all right !' he answered
vaguely, just catching the intonation of
voice that indicated an inquiry; then, removing his arm from her waist, he threw
himself forward, with his broad back bent
and his elbows resting on his knees. Gertie,
looking at him sidelong, saw that his eyes
were fixed on the waving poplars, whose
shining leaves rustled ceaselessly in the
breeze. His lips were tightly compressed
and his nostrils expanded. There was
something in his face which filled the wife's
jealous heart with an exultant belief that,
however fond he had been at one time of
his cousin, he was displeased to renew the
acquaintance.

' Well, we must get rid of her somehow !'
he muttered, recovering himself suddenly;
and then, rising to his feet, he asked once
again, ' Where is she ?'

'In the library, dear. Miss Drummond wished her boxes to be sent for; and Philippe brought them in the light cart.'

'Ah, then he can take 'em back again in the light cart! What's o'clock—half-past five? What time have you fixed for dinner?'

'Six.'

'I'll tell Louise to put it back as I go through the house. It's all right, Gertie. You go and stroll in the forest till I come and find you; take Pierce with you. I have a fancy for some wood-strawberries; see if you can find me some.'

He kissed her, and walked off under the veranda and into the house, with his hands in his pockets. Gertie sat down, wondering what her husband's intentions were, yet with a wonderful feeling of relief and a grateful sense of reliance in his strength and wisdom.

Presently Pierce came out, carrying a flower-basket and a garden-hat for her mistress.

The admirable woman's features were a little more pinched than usual—the only sign that ever betrayed disinclination to a service required of her. Gertie searched the banks until her basket was half full of strawberries and she felt fatigued; then she sat down within sight of the house, and waited for Gilbert's coming.

When at length he appeared upon the path leading up into the forest, she dismissed Pierce, and went forward to meet him.

His eyes were upon the ground, yet to the wife's eager observation there appeared, even at that distance, a look upon his face which alarmed her. Perhaps there had been an unpleasant scene between him and his cousin. He quickened his step and smiled as he caught sight of her.

' I've been a long time, Gertie, haven't I?' he said, taking her hand and passing it under his arm. ' The fact is, I undertook a task that just goes beyond my power. I've been trying all this time to get her to go, and she won't.'

' I don't see why you set yourself the task, dear.'

' Oh, that's easily enough explained ! She's vulgar and coarse; and there's not a single pleasant quality in her.'

A sigh of satisfaction escaped from Gertie. She found herself looking at Miss Drummond's visit in a much more cheerful spirit now.

' Miss Drummond has the good taste to

like your society, or she wouldn't have been
so anxious to stay—that's one merit,' she
said, laughing.

'I wish she had the good taste to leave a
house where she sees she's not wanted,'
Gilbert rejoined uneasily.

'Perhaps she did not see it. You couldn't
be rude to a lady; and I don't think you
could try to be.'

'No, that's it, you know,' he said, catching at the excuse quickly. 'A man can
say straight out what he thinks to another
man; but it's different with a woman,
isn't it ?'

'Certainly, dear. And I don't see why
you should wish to get rid of Miss Drummond—at once. Variety, even if it isn't
quite the kind one most likes, is pleasant.
Here you have no one to talk to but me,
and you may find it agreeable to gossip

with some one you have known formerly about old times, and so on.'

At another time Gilbert would have laughed heartily at his wife's thinly-veiled jealousy; now he replied in a serious vein, telling her that he had no wish to talk of old times, but preferred to live entirely in the better age that had begun with his marriage. It pleased Gertie to hear that, though she had heard it before; and, pressing his arm in grateful acknowledgment, she continued, with still rising spirits :

'It was wrong to say anything to prejudice you against your cousin; I did not mean to do so. I only feared that I might appear rather insignificant and silly, sitting beside that large handsome woman who talks so freely and fluently.'

'Heaven preserve you from ever having

anything in common with that woman!' Gilbert said, with fervour.

'Don't you think you judge her rather severely, dear? A great many people who strike us at first as being not quite nice reveal, after a while, certain qualities that command respect, and sometimes admiration.'

'To be sure they do. And, even if this woman doesn't improve, I dare say we can manage to put up with her vulgarity and unpleasantness for a few weeks. At the end of that time, if she doesn't run away from us, we can manage to run away from her—take another cruise in the *Tub*, or something of that sort.'

'I don't think we shall have to do that; at least, I hope not, unless you quite wish it.' She had pictured her baby learning its first steps on the smooth lawn among the flowers and sweet surroundings of this house, and the vision was too delightful to abandon readily. 'I think I shall like Miss Drummond when I know her better; I shall certainly do all I can to make her like me. Besides, we shall find many opportunities of being alone together, you and I. I should think she would soon get tired of our quiet ways. At all events, she must leave us some day.'

Gilbert shrugged his shoulders, with a short uneasy laugh, and then became suddenly stern as the turn of the path brought into sight the house, with Miss Drummond seated under the veranda and displaying a liberal extent of scarlet silk stocking.

Gertie had never seen on her husband's face such a morose expression; but, with

Miss Drummond's red stocking and her large bare white arms and shoulders flashing in the distance, she would possibly have been less contented to see her husband looking otherwise.

CHAPTER III.

CORRESPONDENCE.—THE MESHES BEGIN TO CLOSE ABOUT SIR GILBERT.

From Mrs. Pierce, Fontainebleau, to Mrs. Gower, London.

'July 23, 188—.

'DEAR MADAM,

'Since writing to acknowledge receipt of cheque, events have occurred which justify the conclusion we had drawn, and fully realize the hopes with which our proceedings have been planned. I am happy to inform you that Sophia Kirby arrived here last Thursday, introducing herself as Miss Drummond and the cousin of Sir Gilbert Linton. You possibly know whether Sir G. has any such relative bearing that name.

' Her appearance coincides exactly with the description furnished by my partner in London, from information obtained in the neighbourhood of Monkden, and with the general particulars furnished by you, excepting that the woman's hair is light in colour, instead of dark. This discrepancy is easily accounted for by the bottles of washes and dyes which I have found in her boxes, and which I have positive knowledge she uses night and morning. Her conversation and manners agree entirely with the supposition that she is Sophia Kirby. She has the character of a servant and the dress of a princess. In her boxes I have failed to find any letters or documents to prove her identity. Her linen is unmarked. Her jewellery consists of two watches, one set with seed-pearls and one with fifty small diamonds; three chains, one cable Albert, one nine long-link Albert (gold), one long delicately chased lady's chain (gold), interspersed with cat's-eyes; superb spray for the hair, representing a clove pink in rubies, emeralds, and diamonds; garniture, consisting of necklet, pendant and ear-rings in emerald and diamonds, set in French gold; five pairs of ear-rings, the most remarkable being two single rose diamonds of large size and extraordinary lustre, with spring fastenings, in English gold; ten bracelets, seed-pearl and turquoise—diamonds and rubies—filigree silver—plain silver; antique cameos, long, and each surrounded with diamonds; bangles, silver, gold, and gold set with sapphires; a square box, antique, eight inches long, six broad, and five deep, solid silver studded with gems, locked, and not to be opened by ordinary means, heavy, and, by the sound when shaken, containing stones and loose trinkets.

'You may be able to tell me whether you identify any of these articles with the late Lady Linton's jewels. A silver-mounted revolver, bearing the name of a Parisian maker, is in all probability a later acquisition. I may mention, while on this subject, that the revolver is charged, showing that the woman has prepared herself for any desperate contingency which may ensue. The boxes contain no further evidence; though perhaps I should mention that a pair of light-blue satin shoes, scarcely soiled, and embroidered with seed-pearls, is amongst the effects, and that the size is No. 2, whereas S. K.'s shoes and boots are all No. 3.

'I will now proceed to give you an account of what has happened. S. K. arrived in the absence of Sir Gilbert, and with the utmost effrontery declared her intention of staying. She did not disguise the contempt she had for Lady L., and adopted an insolent tone in speaking to her, which would have aroused the anger of anyone less naturally amiable than she. She had not been in the house half an hour before she avowed having been in love with Sir Gilbert, and signified that he had been unfaithful to his first wife. She ordered Lady L. to send to Fontaine-bleau for the luggage, and instructed me as to the accommodation and services she required. In fact, it was evident that she had come to the house with the intention of making herself the mistress of it and insulting Lady L.

'Lady L. was at first simply terrified. When she regained composure, she showed herself painfully anxious to disguise her feeling and treat her husband's relative with courtesy. Pending Sir G.'s return, Lady L. entertained her visitor by showing her the house and grounds; afterwards they entered the salon, and I was able to glean a few scraps of their conversation. S. K. seemed anxious to learn all about Lady G.'s engagement, her marriage, and so forth. Lady L. was much embarrassed to reply, and finally said it was a subject on which she could not speak freely even with her most intimate friend. S. K. pretended to be much amused, and adopted a bantering tone, as if she were teasing a child, and, having found out Lady L.'s susceptibilities,

did her utmost to wound them. She signified that Lady L. was a simpleton, a
pretty toy that Sir G. had taken up to clear
away the gloomy thoughts produced by the
loss of his first wife ; and, laughing heartily
when Lady L. defended her husband, declared that he was no better than the rest of
mankind, and might be as unfaithful to his
second wife as he had been to his first. In
a patronizing tone she bade her look at life
not from a schoolgirl's point of view, but
as a woman of the world, who, having
married a man of the world, must put up
with the consequences as the price to be
paid for the material advantages she had
obtained.

'Lady L. met her husband on his return
with the most unhappy expression upon
her face which I have yet seen there. They
consulted privately, and the result was that

Lady L.'s manner entirely changed, and I concluded that Sir G. had promised to dismiss his visitor. He then went into the library to meet S. K. What occurred then I was unfortunately prevented from over-hearing; the upshot, however, completely overthrew my expectations, for S. K. re-mained, and is now finally established here. This is conclusive that she holds Sir G. under her thumb. Her behaviour is in-sulting, both to Sir G. and his wife. She calls the former "Bertie," and the latter "Baby;" she makes love to Sir G. before his wife's face, kisses him when they meet in the morning and part at night, exercising, as she says, her "cousinly right." She refers frequently to Sir G.'s first wife, with equivocal allusions to their connection at the Abbey, which must cut Sir G. and his wife also to the quick. It is clear that he suffers more on Lady L.'s account than on his own; his haggard look shows how much. Yet he suffers that woman to torment him, and to make the wife he loves so tenderly wretched to the most intense degree, and this at a time when she expects to be a mother. Would he suffer this torture to continue if " Miss Drummond " and Sophia Kirby were not one and the same person, or if he had not been that Sophia Kirby's accomplice in the murder of his wife? His submission to S. K. is the price of her silence. He dare not break his present relations with her, for that would destroy the sole advantage S. K. has in being silent. She would take her revenge at once by exposing all ; that exposure would separate husband and wife at once. *Lady Linton could not live with a man who had murdered his first wife to make her his second.*

If I know anything of her character, *she would leave him, and give up every single thing she has received from his hands. He knows this; he knows that such an imprudent rupture with S. K. would cause the death of his wife and their unborn child.*

'The only means of escaping such a calamity is in flight, and this, I feel sure, Sir Gilbert is meditating. S. K. is not blind to this possibility, and she has already taken precautions to assure herself a clue by which to pursue them. She has given me several valuable presents, and last night she said to me, as I was arranging her hair for the night, " It is my custom, Pierce, at the end of a visit to give twenty or fifty guineas, as the case may be, to the lady's-maid who attends to my little wants. But, as it is just likely that Sir Gilbert, in his eccentric way, may carry off his wife to the other end of the world and take you with her—and that without intimation—you are likely to lose the proper remuneration for your services. I should be very sorry for that to occur ; and so, if you do go away, I beg you to write a little line to me, saying where you are, that I may send the money on to you. You will oblige me very much by doing this. May I rely on you ?" I promised, of course, and you may be sure, madam, that I intend to keep my promise. I have taken pains to show you the exact position of affairs, because I wish you to have faith in our action, and also because I wish you to co-operate with us in bringing this case not only to a private confirmation of our suspicions, but to a public conviction of the guilty parties. We have sufficient evidence already of Sir Gilbert's complicity with Sophia Kirby ; but it is entirely pre-

sumptive, and I believe it would be quite
impossible to obtain the arrest and extradi-
tion of Sir G. and S. K. upon that evidence.
With patience, we may obtain—and shall, I
firmly believe—evidence of a much more
convincing kind. S. K. is playing into our
hands. Prompted by jealousy and hatred,
she will carry her insults beyond bearing.
The rupture that Sir G. now fears must
come if this system of persecution continues ;
there will be an open denunciation at which
I shall find means to be present, and my
testimony will be sufficient to obtain a
warrant for the arrest of Sir Gilbert and
Sophia Kirby. You may be sure, madam,
that I shall do all that is in my power to
hasten the catastrophe.

‘ Your obedient servant,

‘ E. PIERCE.

'P.S.—It has occurred to me, since writing the above, that possibly Mr. Gower might serve as an instrument to the open disclosure of Sophia Kirby's identity, if you choose to employ him for that purpose. Undoubtedly in his visits to Monkden Abbey he encountered S. K. Her appearance is sufficiently striking to remain in a man's memory. If he were brought face to face with her, I feel sure I could discover by his expression whether he had seen her before or not ; moreover, her behaviour and Sir Gilbert's would be indicative. Such a recognition would be of the utmost importance when Mr. Gower takes his place in the witness-box. Lady L. is in constant communication with Mrs. Simpson, of Kennington, from whom Mr. Gower would learn her place of residence, even if Sir Gilbert does not correspond with him.

I beg to suggest—as a means of procuring his evidence—that you should desire him to go with you to Paris, taking your daughters with you. When there, you will find an excuse to return to London precipitately, leaving your family in Paris. The strong affection of Mr. Gower and his daughters for Lady L. will in all probability prompt them to make a hasty visit to Fontainebleau in your absence. I shall be glad to know if you approve of this suggestion, that I may make my plans accordingly.'

* * * * *

From Mrs. Gower, London, to Mrs. Pierce, Fontainebleau.

'Mrs. Gauntly Gower agrees with E. Pierce in every particular, and feels increased reliance in the ability of Messrs. Pierce and Pierce. Mrs. Gower identifies all the articles of jewellery described as the property of her daughter, the late Lady Linton. The embroidered slippers are also most likely stolen property, the late Lady L. always wearing "twos." E. Pierce's suggestion relative to Mr. Gower shall be carried out, as soon as business arrangements will permit him to take a holiday. Mrs. Gauntly Gower encloses a cheque in payment of Messrs. Pierce and Pierce's services up to the end of the current month.

'Gauntly House,
'*July* 25, 188—.'

CHAPTER IV.

MISS DRUMMOND MAKES A PROPOSAL TO SIR GILBERT

GERTIE had never been careless with regard to dress ; indeed, Gilbert had often accused her of coquetterie in the pains she took to deck her pretty little person to advantage ; and that accusation pleased her, for she saw that the fact pleased him. But since Miss Drummond's arrival she had spent more time than ever at her toilette, and found it never before so difficult to satisfy herself.

At length she complained to him that she had not really a dress fit to wear in the evening ; and he, laughing, declared that in that case the sooner they went to Paris and bought one that was fit, the better it would be. She accepted the suggestion joyfully. For a whole day at least she should have her husband all to herself; they could talk without restriction, and there would be no terrible Miss Drummond to fear.

The very next morning they started for Paris, giving their visitor only a quarter of an hour's notice of their intention. They lunched at the Maison Dorée ; they had a delicious drive in the Bois ; in the evening they went to the Folies Dramatiques, and Gertie was the happiest, gayest soul in Paris. The next morning Gilbert left her with MM. Worth et Cie., and bade her find

him in the Cluny Museum in three hours'
time. After a long and serious consultation,
Gertie selected a dress, and went through
the necessary measurements. She wished
it to be made in the very latest fashion.
The dressmaker suggested a new pair of
corsets, as waists were being worn small;
whereupon Gertie procured herself an in-
genious machine for contracting her supple
and delicate figure into the form of a balloon-
neck, and left the establishment with a sigh
of satisfaction and an exultant anticipation
of the day when she should sit down to
dinner in that corset with Miss Drummond.
She turned back to assure herself that
MM. Worth et Cie. fully understood that,
unless the dress were sent to her in a week
at the latest, it would be of no use to her
whatever. MM. Worth fully understood
her—perhaps in another sense to that she

intended—and begged her to be quite at
ease ; they never disappointed their customers.

In seven days the dress was delivered ;
it fitted her to perfection when the corsets
had done their work. And now Gertie
was prepared to go down into the salon
and triumph over Miss Drummond. Even
the frigid Pierce had been moved to
admiration by her appearance, expressing
herself in correctly respectful terms.

Gertie dismissed her with a smile, and
was about to go downstairs, when she
fancied it would do her good to sit down
by the window for a moment or two. She
felt the necessity of air. She did not
breathe quite freely ; there was an oppression about her heart as if it could not beat
easily. She had felt just such a sensation
before under the influence of very strong

emotion. She was naturally anxious about the success of this dress—that was it. If she sat down and composed her feelings, the unpleasant oppression would pass off.

Pierce had opened the windows and closed the persiennes before leaving the room, so admitting the fresh air and shutting out the brilliant light. That was exactly what Gertie wanted. Sitting by the window, she could see the level green lawn, with its beds of bright geraniums and heliotrope, whose penetrating perfume floated into the room.

Gilbert had been more gloomy than ever since the happy days in Paris. How careworn he looked, and how absent his thoughts were at times! It was a long while since he had taken notice of her dress; at one time his eyes detected the slightest change. Would he remark the dress she wore to-day, and look happier because it became her so well ?

Probably Miss Drummond would be more hateful than ever, and offer some coarse personal observation to make her appear ridiculous to her husband. Gertie didn't care—she knew that no dress could be lovelier or more fashionable; and if it didn't show quite so great a quantity of arms and neck as Miss Drummond's dresses, it showed enough to prove that they were quite as white and as finely shaped as hers. One thing was clear—if it displeased Miss Drummond, it would be because she feared it would please Gilbert.

Her position at the window gave her a view of the farther half of the lawn ; the nearer half was cut off by the deflexure of the persiennes. Suddenly the very people she was thinking about came into her field of view

Gilbert came first. His back was to her. His head was bent, his hands were crossed behind him ; he was walking slowly. Evidently he had strolled out from the house.

After him came Miss Drummond, in her horrid pink satin ; she was walking quickly, clearly bent on overtaking him. Gertie's fingers twitched nervously at her corsage as she watched. Miss Drummond overtook Gilbert, and slipped her arm under his. Ah, he did not take his hands from behind, and simply suffered her to cling to his arm ! With that affectation of arch playfulness which so disgusted Gertie, Miss Drummond lifted her fan with her disengaged hand and tapped Gilbert's cheek. He walked stolidly onward. She

let her fan drop by her side, and, clasping
her hands together upon his arm, leant
towards him until her face almost touched
his shoulder. Her nasty, scented little
frizzy curls must be quite in his dear face.
He spoke to her, disengaging his arm from
her embrace. She laughed, turning her
head quickly to glance back at the house.
It was that insolent laugh that stabbed
Gertie's heart ; she was not jealous—why
should she be ? The advances were
always on this woman's side ; they an-
noyed Gilbert. He had clearly told her
that he didn't like to be hugged in that
way ; perhaps he had said that her inde-
cent behaviour might be seen from the
house. And that laugh had shown how
little she cared for the people in the house
and what they suffered.

They passed out of the range of her

view; Gertie could only follow their move-
ments by rising from her seat. They took
the path leading up into the forest—Gilbert
with his hands in his pockets now, and she
once more clinging to his arm.

'He will give his dear arm to me,'
thought Gertie, and, thinking no more
about the difficulty of breathing and the
oppression at her heart, she hurried downstairs and through the salon, determined to
show that horrid woman that she commanded her husband's respect by means
of no artifice, and held his love in spite
of her.

Pierce was arranging the chairs in the
salon.

'Will your ladyship have the goodness
to give me the key of the cellar, that
Philippe may get the wine for dinner?'
she asked.

Gertrude thought she had given Pierce the keys before going upstairs, and it took quite five minutes before she found that she had laid them on the casement where she had been sitting.

Gilbert and Miss Drummond had not returned. She crossed the lawn and followed the path into the fir-wood without seeing them. Probably Gilbert had gone to his favourite seat on the other side of the wood, which commanded a view of the Seine in the magnificent sweep below Thomery. Often and often she and he had gone there together; she knew the short cut through the firs, and made in a straight line for the point. The dry brown pine-needles formed a smooth carpet under her feet that made her step noiseless. Only the rustling of the oak scrub that bordered the fir-wood broke the silence.

'After all, I'm what you have made me.'

The words fell with startling distinctness upon Gertie's ear ; and, turning her head as she stopped abruptly, she saw them close to her—Gilbert with his back against a tree and his face turned towards the distant hills, Miss Drummond seated on the stump of a cut fir, a few feet from him.

Gertie put her hand upon the bole of a fir for support. The ascent of the hill had made her strangely giddy, and it seemed as if each beat of her heart would suffocate her. It was Miss Drummond who spoke. Gilbert made no response. After a few moments of silence, she continued :

'Whatever I am, I deserve your consideration. If you have done your best to make me hate you, you have also done your best to make me love you ; and, if you have succeeded, you have no right to blame me, however late my love has come. You know I love you.'

'It is you who say so.'

'I say so. Well, can you deny it? Would any woman in my position, without my love, have been so merciful?'

He laughed contemptuously.

'I have been merciful!' she continued, with emphasis. ' What but mercy has made me hold my tongue?'

'Prudence.'

'Prudence! What advantage have I gained by silence? All that you had to give you offered me at Cherbourg, and I refused it. Was that prudence? Tell me what I have to gain by keeping silent.'

' There's your life to lose by not keeping silent.'

' Oh, do you think I wish to die of old

age? I'd blow out my brains to-morrow if I found a wrinkle in my face.'

'There's nothing particularly new and interesting in what you say. If you have told me all you wished to tell, we will return to the house.'

'I've not finished yet. When I agreed to play my part in the farce that has been running here for the last three or four weeks, I suppressed a very strong inclination to be revenged on that bit of a girl who has taken my place; and for that sacrifice I expected a reward. You ought to know that I am not the kind of woman whose fad is self-sacrifice. I never did believe that virtue was its own reward, nor anything like it. If you thought I should rest content to be a visitor in the house which should be mine, and to witness another receiving those caresses to which I have the first claim, you were mistaken. I expected at least to share your caresses— I tell you that, that you may know how to reconcile me to the position you wish me to retain. I am flesh and blood, Gilbert ; I am a woman with rather more than a woman's share of passion and jealousy, and I tell you that the present condition of things is intolerable. I can read that stupid child's face, and I know the meaning of her gaiety to-day : she has a dress to wear at dinner to-day which she thinks it will mortify me to see. She is right—for you gave it to her.'

'I'll give you a dozen as good, you know, for the asking.'

'I don't choose to ask.'

'Ah, and all this business is because the poor girl has a new dress—eh?'

'Whether it is that or something else

doesn't matter. The result is that I am
resolved that this state of things shall end.'

' Yes.   Have you any alteration to
suggest?'

She paused.   Gilbert continued to look
with a dull eye on the golden hills.

Gertie had listened like one in a dream,
who has a vague futile wish to get away
or not to hear.   She dared not move, for
fear of falling—it seemed as if the tree she
held rocked to and fro with the landscape
before her eyes, and that the earth was
slipping, slipping, slipping away from her
feet.   Now and then a pang shot through
her body, as if a knife were being thrust into
her, and she had to bite her lip to prevent
a cry escaping ; and then a cold moisture
broke out upon her forehead, and there was
a sickness at her heart, and her limbs
trembled so that each moment she expected

to lose her hold upon the tree and fall. Oh, if she could only get away without being seen or heard !

'You must send that maudlin child away ! That is what it must come to, sooner or later.' Gertie heard that, and summoned her courage with the desperate resolution of getting down the hill before that pain came again. 'You will throw her aside, as you threw me aside.'

A dull thud, like the sound of a log falling on the turf, reached Gilbert's ear above the harsh raking voice of Miss Drummond ; and, turning his head, he saw his wife lying face downwards on the earth.

CHAPTER V

GERTIE'S swoon was not of long duration. When consciousness returned she found her head upon Gilbert's shoulder ; she felt that he was carrying her, and that they were descending the hill. Something terrible had happened, she could not remember what. It was delightful to know that she was in his arms, and to yield to the desire to close her eyes and forget again.

Presently she felt something cold upon

her temples, so cold that it took her breath away, and, opening her eyes, she discovered that she was lying upon the ground, with her head resting in the hollow of her husband's arm, and that he was dipping a handkerchief in the watercourse by which she lay. He wetted her temples, and she remembered that she had fallen giddy under the firs. How tenderly he cared for her !

'Dear one !' she murmured, lifting her arm and drawing his hand to her lips.

'Better now ?' he asked.

'Oh yes ! I could sit up, love.' She thought of her new dress, and feared the water would spoil it.

He raised her to a sitting posture, supporting her firmly. She felt the water trickle from her face, and looked down at her dress in alarm. The wonderful bodice was cut from the top to the bottom, and, beneath, her corsets gaped open, cut equally from top to bottom.

' Oh, my beautiful dress !' she cried.

' Good God, Gertie !' exclaimed Gilbert, with impatience. ' Don't you know that the thing might have killed you ? What on earth induced you to put yourself in such an infernal machine as that ?'

' Does it displease you, dear?' she asked piteously.

' Heavens ! Do you think to please me by putting yourself on a level with fools— and—and——' He did not complete the sentence.

And this was the result of her plans to win his admiration, and the end of all those hopes she had cherished during the week. She burst into tears, being too

weak to bear her bitter disappointment
with fortitude.

Without a word, Gilbert lifted her up
in his arms and continued his march towards the house.

'He thinks I am nothing but a little
fool, and he will love me no more,' she
thought, with that extravagant despon-
dency which usually follows such a crisis
as that she had gone through.

Then she suddenly recollected what she
had heard on the hill. That woman had
told Gilbert that she was a silly child, and
that he would throw her aside when he
was wearied of her. Was that all a
calumny? Was there not truth in it?
Had she not at this very moment proved
that she was silly? He had listened to
what that bad woman said against her
without angry protest; he had not kissed

her since she returned to life ; he had
seen her burst into tears without attempt-
ing to charm them away with his
sympathy.

Was it not a proof that he thought her
no better than a little fool, and despised her
for her folly ?   And was it not a truth ?
Was she not a fool to let him see now how
weak and wretched she felt ?   He might
suppose that she was crying because her
dress was spoiled.   Oh, she must do something to prove that she was sensible and
strong !

'I am quite myself again now, love,'
she said, bringing her voice under control
by a strong effort.   'I should like to walk;
it will do me good.'

Gilbert set her upon her feet and drew
a long breath ; with all his strength he had
not the superhuman powers of a hero of

romance, and the descent of the hill had tried him.

She drew the cut edges of her bodice together as well as she could, and held them with her hands; and Gilbert, supporting her body with his arm, led her under the shadow of the acacias round the lawn to the house. His silence frightened her. How could she convince him that she was not a silly child?

'I haven't heard the bell yet,' she said, trying to speak in an ordinary tone, as if nothing had happened. 'I may not keep dinner waiting, after all.'

'Oh, hang the dinner! Time enough for that when we've got you to bed.'

Gertie submitted without remonstrance, saying to herself that it would be a poor sign of good sense to oppose herself to her husband's wisdom.

She felt better lying down, with the cool pillow under her head, which ached a little. Gilbert drew the curtains and kissed her before he went away. She wished to speak to him; she did not know what she had to say, but there was a load at her heart which would be removed if only she could pour out its care to him. But Pierce was in the room, and it was impossible. When he was gone, she sat up in bed and said:

'Pierce, take away that dress, and the corsets as well. I don't want to see them ever again—do you understand?'

'Yes, madam. Does your ladyship require anything else?' The careful woman was anxious to know what was going on at the dinner-table.

'No. If I want anything at all, I will ring for you.'

Left to herself, Gertie determined to think it all out rationally, and determine what her line of conduct should be. But her ideas would not arrange themselves—there were so many all hurrying through her mind that they upset each other, as it were; and somehow the rustling of the poplars by the river and the scent of heliotrope wafting through the persiennes got the ascendancy over everything else, and she fell asleep.

It was quite dark when she awoke. Her headache had passed off, and she felt refreshed and invigorated by her long sleep. She remembered now quite clearly all that had taken place from the time she put on her dress to the time she bade Pierce carry it away. Everything came before her with marvellous distinctness; even the phrases she had caught as she stood under the firs, with that sickening pain in her heart. What she had heard of the dialogue between Miss Drummond and Gilbert had not caused her to faint away. She had heard little that she had not before learnt or surmised. Gilbert had been Miss Drummond's lover once upon a time. Miss Drummond told her that the very first day she came; and, unpleasant as the fact was, she had reconciled herself to it as a thing of the past, which could not be undone by idle regrets.

The secret she referred to was their liaison, no doubt. It was horrible to think that Gilbert had really loved that woman; but she must make allowances for him. She knew now that men and women were not governed by the same code of morals, and that what would be a crime in the latter was but a fault in the former, which

every one in society recognised as a kind
of privilege due to their sex—to be smiled
at rather than censured.

Perhaps Miss Drummond was nice when
she was younger, and less coarse and
sensual looking, and poor Gilbert had no
one to love in that dismal old Abbey, for
his wife was no wife at all to him. He
did not love her now, that was very certain,
and he never could again.

Oh, he would never cease to love her
who was his real wife, if she only bore
herself bravely, kept bright and pleasant,
and didn't do foolish things ! It was the
knowledge of that which made Miss Drummond so angry. He would never, never,
never yield to her horrid wishes. Where
was he now ? What time was it ?

With this thought she drew back the
curtain of her bed, to see if any light was

showing through the window. It took her
a moment or two to make out what she
saw.

Ah, the window was open and the persiennes thrown back—that was how the
beauty of the starry heavens came to be before her eyes. Gilbert perhaps had come to
look at her before going to bed in the next
room, and had opened the window, the
night being so still and calm. As she
looked, a great dark figure rose against the
sky.

'Oh, is it you, my darling?' she cried,
recognising, even in the darkness, the form
of her husband's head and body.

'Awake, Gertie?' he said, coming to
her.

She could not speak; her heart was so
full of love and of joy to think he should
be watching in her room while she slept;

but she drew him down to her and kissed his lips and his face.

'Feel all right again, sweetheart ?' he asked, resting himself by her side on the bed.

'Oh, yes—yes, quite, love !' She was grateful for the darkness, for tears—she knew not why—had sprung to her eyes, and were silently flowing down her cheek on to the pillow. 'Is it late, dear ?' she added in a whisper, that the sound of her voice might not betray her.

'The old bear's getting jolly low down.'

'And my favourites, the pleiades, where are they ?' ·

'Oh, right away out there !' Gilbert extended his arm; then brought it back and stroked her hair gently with his fingers.

Now she was nearly happy. She would talk without being silly.

'I've sent them away, dear,' she said, in a light confidential undertone.

'What—the seven stars?'

'No—my dress and the corsets. I didn't think they would displease you.'

'Of course you didn't. I know all about it. You would wear rags with the same purpose. Do you think I haven't read the riddle of that dress? Poor little Gertie, putting her body to the torture for the sake of a smile, and getting no return for her loving tribute but a harsh rebuke!'

'I deserved it, dear. It was very silly to do that.'

'If that was silly, then they were fools, and nothing more, whose devotion led them to the rack. Did I seem very cruel, Gertie?'

'How could you seem cruel, dear, to me?'

'Men are sometimes cruel from mere want of self-command, or perhaps from a kind of brutal instinct to punish those who give them pain. I dare say, if I analysed my feeling, I should find that I was angry with you for having risked so much for my sake. Fancy what might have happened! —then I was upset, to begin with—worried beyond endurance by that woman, you know.'

'Why do you let her worry you, love?'

'Because I can't help myself. We were having a kind of explanation when you were coming to us.'

'I was going away, dear. I didn't want to hear what you were saying.'

'Ah, you heard something, then?'

'Yes, something.'

There was perfect silence for a minute. His fingers ceased to stroke her hair.

'What did you hear?' he asked then, in a low earnest tone.

'I heard her threaten to reveal something which you had made her promise to keep secret, and that explained why you had tolerated her stay with us. But I don't think you need mind that, love, if you would like to send her away.'

'Mind what, Gertie?'

'Her speaking. I shan't mind it. I think I know the worst.

Again he was silent, as if his courage would not carry him further.

'What do you know?' he said at length. 'Tell me.'

'She told me, before you saw her in the library, on the day of her arrival, that— that you had been sweethearts at the Abbey.'

She paused.

'Go on.'

'And it seemed to me, dear, that perhaps your connection was more serious than that, and consequently she felt that you ought to marry her when your wife's death made you free to do so. Of course she knows how——'

'Gertie,' said he, interrupting her, as though he had not heard her last words. 'You've love enough in that heart of yours to have faith in me?'

'Could I love you if I had not?'

'Perhaps,' he replied, after a pause. 'Yes, I believe your love would outlive your faith. If I were criminal in the eye of the law and of all the world, you would yet love me, wouldn't you?'

'The opinion of all the world wouldn't shake my faith in your love for me, and that is all I want.'

He changed his position, and was silent again for a space.

' That's not exactly what I mean, Gertie —but it's near enough.'

He got up and went to the window, and, leaning on the sill, hummed tunelessly. Gertie was disappointed by this abrupt termination of the conversation. He had seemed on the point of revealing something to her, something that would require the firmest faith in his love to forgive, perhaps ; and in her mind she had accepted the trust joyfully, confident that with a little struggle she could overcome her jealousy, and that thenceforward there would be no secret, and the future would be clear and cloudless.

But now he shrank from the subject, she thought, possibly disgusted with the vulgarity and unpleasantness of it, and seemed to think that, if she had faith in him, that was all that was required, and that things might be permitted to take their natural course.

'The sky is growing light over Vulaines,' he said, when he turned from the window; 'the dawn's at hand.'

He closed the persiennes, kissed his wife, and spoke a few kind words, drew the curtains of her bed, and left her.

CHAPTER VI.

ERTIE went down to luncheon the following morning fully expecting to be punished by Miss Drummond for her folly. It is such an easy thing to inflict pain on those who are conscious of having acted unwisely; and here was such an admirable opportunity for showing Gilbert how unfitted his wife was for the grade of society in which he had placed her.

She might assume a lofty tone of pity,

or she might couch her venomous sarcasms
in the form of badinage—no matter how,
she would certainly employ all her powers
to mortify her and make her ridiculous
before Gilbert. Gertie was undaunted—
Gilbert had given her new courage—and
she would show him how much love for
him and what faith in his love she had
by going unflinchingly through any ordeal
to which she was subjected. She would
keep her temper—she would not forget
that she was Gilbert's wife and a lady;
she would bear herself with dignity and
as much composure as it was possible for
her to command.

What harm was there in all Miss
Drummond's sneers and taunts if Gilbert
loved her all the while? Surely he would
love her the more for meeting persecution
bravely! And she would keep repeating

to herself, whenever she felt the need of support:

'There's love enough in that heart of yours to have faith in me.'

Those were his words.

But, as not unfrequently happens in this world of surprises, that which was expected did not occur.

Miss Drummond was absolutely silent with regard to the event in the fir wood, not a single innuendo or unpleasant insinuation escaped her. But, seeming to see that an apology was necessary for her lack of spirit, she said, posing her thumb and third finger on her delicately pencilled eyebrows:

'I have an awful headache this morning, Baby, positively awful. Not a word to throw at a dog. You will understand my silence, I am sure.'

That was exactly what Gertie could not do at first. Miss Drummond was not unfrequently afflicted with headache in the morning; but it was usually marked by an increased acerbity of temper and a free expression of it.

'Would you like any remedy fetched from Fontainebleau? May I send for a doctor?' asked Gertie.

'No, thanks. I have to go over to Fontainebleau on business, and the drive will do me good. I will have the dog-cart, if you are not going to use it, Baby.'

Marvel on marvel! This was the first time she had ever consulted anyone's convenience but her own in ordering what she wanted.

'Only too happy to place it at your disposition in any circumstances,' replied

Gertie; and the brightness of her eyes testified to the truth of her assertion. ‘ Pierce will take your orders.’

Miss Drummond issued her commands languidly, and, protesting she could not eat anything, unfolded her serviette and arranged the glasses before her. Now, indeed, Gertie shone as a hostess, and, with only such help as she got from Gilbert, who was not very talkative this morning, she contrived to keep up a little flow of conversation and gossip which sparkled now and then with happy flashes of womanly wit, and was pleasant to listen to all through.

Miss Drummond scarcely opened her lips to speak during the lunch, not even to complain; but she managed to eat a little of everything upon the table and left very little at the bottom of her bottle of champagne. Now and then she raised her narrow eyes to glance furtively from Gilbert to Gertrude, and returned them without change of expression to her plate.

'If it is all the same to you, I will take coffee in my own room, Baby,' she said, rising from the table when she had finished dessert.

It was not at all the same to Gertie; but she hid her satisfaction as well as she could and replied with propriety; then, as Miss Drummond swept from the room, she heaved a deep sigh of satisfaction and smiled at her husband.

They went on to the terrace, and had coffee served under the veranda. Gilbert lit his pipe, and Gertie, with her hands in her lap and a happy curve in her lips, leaned back in her chair and mused.

'What is it, Gertie?' asked Gilbert,

leaning forward, his arms resting on his knees.

She recovered herself and turned to him with a little laugh—Miss Drummond's room happily was at the other end of the house; she did not fear the consequences of laughing.

'What are you thinking about?' he asked.

'Nothing at all of any importance. It's odd how things sometimes come into one's mind that are quite out of keeping with the subject one has at heart! Do you know, I was thinking of a show that used to stand near Kennington Church every Saturday night.'

'What sort of show?'

'Oh, a most melancholy exhibition of all sorts of animals put together in one large cage! A happy family, the man used to call them, poor things! But the creature that is most conspicuous in my memory was an old, old cat with a poor miserable tail and two green eyes, that used to crouch in a corner with her ears laid back and divide her attention between a sparrow hopping about within the cage and a most brutal-looking man on the outside, who pointed out the marvels of his collection with a long, thin, sharp-pointed iron skewer.'

'Don't need a conjuror to interpret that vision, Gertie. You're the sparrow, Miss Drummond the cat with the green eyes. and I'm the brute with the skewer.'

Gertie was astonished. After all, it may have been Miss Drummond's unnatural mildness, something of stealthiness and latent cruelty in her eyes when they were at their most quiescent state, which

had brought this memory into existence.
But certainly nothing in Gilbert's appearance had brought that horrid man before
her. Why had he compared himself to
him?

Gilbert smiled tranquilly, watching with
pleasure the expression on his wife's pretty
face as she mentally unravelled the skein he
had set before her.

'Isn't it a headache?' she asked suddenly,
guessing at the truth.

Gilbert shook his head.

'What have you done?'

'Had it out with her. Made her understand that she should torture you and me
no more. Bade her go away and do her
worst, or stay here and do her best. She
has shown by her behaviour at luncheon
which she prefers to do. And she's wise.
She could have made us exceedingly un-

happy—only for a time, I believe; but the consequences would have been still more unpleasant for herself.'

'You don't wish to tell me what those consequences for us would be?'

'No, Gertie. I would rather have this hand of mine cut off, and rather this were my last pipe, than let you know. And now put some sugar in my coffee, sweetheart, and let us settle how we're to spend this day happily.'

They spent the afternoon in a punt under the shadow of rustling leaves. Gilbert fishing, Gertie pretending to fish. The fish were not voracious that afternoon, but Gilbert was content to smoke and drop his line in likely places, while Gertie was supremely happy, with her float amongst the reeds and her hook securely fastened in the weeds under the surface, to be alone and near her beloved husband, and to dream of the future.

They dined alone, a telegram from Miss Drummond informing them that she might be detained at Fontainebleau until late. Gertie was not at all curious to know what the business was; only she hoped it might not be hurried through. At ten o'clock Miss Drummond was still absent.

'Better go to bed now, Gertie!' said Gilbert. 'I will receive Miss Drummond when she arrives.'

'She will not think me wanting in courtesy, dear?' suggested Gertie.

'No, no. Go.'

It was after eleven when Gertie heard the sound of wheels and voices. It sounded almost as if some one were singing—but that couldn't be! A little later she heard

voices below—her husband's—speaking in
a low firm authoritative tone, Pierce's in
short incisive phrases, and Miss Drummond's training languorously with occa-
sional bursts of incoherent remonstrance;
then there were sounds upon the marble
floor of the vestibule, as if some weighty
thing were being drawn or pushed forward,
which after a time ended, and only the dis-
contented murmuring of Miss Drummond
was audible. Then a few sharp decisive
words from Gilbert, and a renewal of the
slipping and shuffling of feet upon the floor
of the vestibule, and the sharp opening of a
door—the library door it seemed; then the
sounds went from the vestibule, and simply
the hum of voices from a distant room
reached Gertie's perplexed ear.

Some one tapped at the door.

'Come in,' cried Gertie, sitting up.

Pierce entered, with a pillow upon her arm.

' Sir Gilbert desired me to inform your ladyship that Miss Drummond is unwell, but that there is no necessity for madam to descend,' she said.

Later on, when Gilbert came up, Gertie asked for information. He said evasively:

' Nothing serious — an attack of the nerves, or something in that way. She had a headache before starting, you know. She's lying on the couch in the library; Pierce will stay by her. If she's not better in the morning, we will send for a doctor. But I don't think there will be any necessity for that.'

Then he talked of other matters; and Gertie, seeing that he wished to dismiss the subject, refrained from irritating him with useless questions.

The library was in its ordinary state when Gertie went down the next morning, Miss Drummond being in her room. Pierce reported that she was better, though still suffering severely from headache, and that she desired to keep her room.

Gertie suggested sending Lucas, the groom who had accompanied Miss Drummond the preceding day, to Fontainebleau for the doctor.

'No,' said Gilbert. 'If she needs a doctor she will let us know, you may be sure; there's no false modesty about her. As for Lucas, I have sent him away.'

'Lucas!'

'Yes; dismissed him summarily. The rascal couldn't stand on his legs, he was so tipsy.'

'And Miss Drummond ill! Why, there might have been an accident!'

'There might,' responded Gilbert drily, and in a tone importing that he would have felt very little regret if an accident had occurred.

The following day Miss Drummond came down to luncheon, still suffering from headache, but otherwise showing no sign of her recent attack.

She explained briefly — her head preventing her from talking for long—that she had been with a notary of Fontainebleau to look at a cottage at Samois, and returned feeling 'fearfully out of form;' that she had to wait at the hotel until that horrid groom could be found, and that, to her horror, after starting from Fontainebleau, she discovered that the wretch was intoxicated, and finally that the fright of the journey had acted so violently upon her imagination that she was more dead than alive on reaching home.

The important fact for Gertie in this narrative was that Miss Drummond had been to look at a cottage. When ordinary forms of politeness permitted, she referred to this statement, and timidly asked Miss Drummond if she intended taking a house.

'Yes, Baby. One can't stay here for ever, you know, and I like the neighbourhood too well to leave it. I shall take a little place—if I can find it.'

Miss Drummond stayed in the room the whole day, except at dinner-time. She had a couch drawn into a position where the light was not too offensive, and where she could get a full view of herself in a glass; and there she lay, scarcely moving, save to change one graceful pose for

another, or to dispose her dress more
advantageously to the contour of her
magnificent limbs. She did not read—
she rarely did, unless the newspaper
contained some carefully reported delicious
scandal — and she scarcely spoke, her
tongue being now under the restraint of
good manners.

It suited her indolent sensual nature
to lie, comfortably supported by pillows,
regarding the slight events that passed
and brooding over her own secrets, and
it required a piquant emotion or the
craving of animal appetite to rouse her
from her state of torpor. She watched
Gertie working for an hour at a time
without moving her half-closed eyes; only
when Gilbert came into the room or passed
in the distance her eyes opened a little
wider, the pupils expanded, and they

moved from him to Gertie and back again.

Gilbert, strolling in towards dinner-time, addressed a few cold conventional inquiries to her about the state of her health, and then, sitting down by Gertie, leant forward and chatted with her in a genial undertone. Gertie replied in a few gay words, and continued her stitching. He changed his position to catch her profile, and sat admiring the delicate sweet outline until she detected it, and turned her chair about, smiling with a bright flush of happiness in her cheeks.

Miss Drummond, watching the two through the parted fingers with which she shielded her eyes—she had replied to Gilbert with her eyes closed and her hand in that favourite pose—the thumb and finger on the two brows, so excellently arranged for displaying her arm, the turn of her wrist, and rings—did not fail to see these signs of love; and, had she been ten times a better woman than she was, envy, hatred and malice would have rankled in her heart.

CHAPTER VII.

CORRESPONDENCE.

From Mrs. Pierce, Fontainebleau, to Mrs. Gower, poste restante, Avenue de l'Opera, Paris.

'Valvins, *August* 8, 188—.

' ADAM,

'Obedient to your request, I write to furnish you with full particulars of the visit of Mr. Gower and his daughters. Yesterday morning, while preparing the table for luncheon, I perceived a fly approaching the house by the road from Fontainebleau, and, being apprised by your letter of the probable arrival of Mr. Gower, I went at once to close the drive-gate, which I had purposely left open. The fly had drawn up.

'" Ask the woman if this is the house, Edith," said Mr. Gower.

'Miss Edith Gower put the question to me in French, and, on my replying in English, Mr. Gower asked if Sir Gilbert was at home. I said he was. Mr. Gower paid the driver, and the young ladies, informing me that they wished to take Lady Linton by surprise, asked where they should find her. I replied that she was in the salon with Sir Gilbert, and that they could enter the room by the lawn in front.

'After a little consultation amongst themselves, they proceeded, with suppressed merriment, to approach the house by the lawn, taking the path beside the house, while I entered the house by the door and took a shawl which Sophia Kirby had been unable to find into the salon, in order to see what happened upon the appearance of Mr. Gower.

'Sophia Kirby was lying on a couch, Sir Gilbert was under the veranda, tying some loose sprays of clematis to the trellis. Suddenly Lady Linton dropped the things she was holding in her lap, with an exclamation of pleasure, which was answered by the voices of her visitors.

'Sir Gilbert, on perceiving the cause of these cries, instead of going to meet Mr. Gower and his family, strode into the salon, and was about to speak, when he caught sight of me. He went to Sophia Kirby's side and spoke in a hurried whisper. In a moment she whisked from the couch and slipped out of the room at the very instant Mr. Gower appeared at the window. Thus, madam, the recognition we had hoped for was evaded; nevertheless, the conclusion to be drawn from the incident which did occur is valuable.

'Sophia Kirby had luncheon served in her apartment, pleading indisposition as an excuse for her absence from the diningroom — an excuse which was partly justified by the previous state of her health.

'After luncheon the visitors went over the grounds, and the young ladies explored every room except that in which Sophia Kirby had locked herself, loudly expressing their astonishment and delight at all they saw. The young ladies were very gay and loquacious, and I have never seen

Lady Linton in brighter spirits. After dinner the whole party went upon the water.

'Sophia Kirby, of course, remained in her room. She wrote several letters, which I have not been able to examine.

'When the party returned from boating, Sir Gilbert and Mr. Gower spent a couple of hours in the billiard-room, while Lady Linton and her young friends chatted in the salon — about Mrs. Simpson of Kennington, and facts with which your copy of the diary has acquainted you. It is unnecessary to pain you by repeating the slighting allusions made to you by the Misses Gower and Mr. Gower. Mr. Gower smoked a great many cigars, was particularly merry, and took the spirit-case to bed with him.

'This morning, after very early breakfast, the party left in the break, taking with them a cold luncheon, and a hamper of wine selected by Mr. Gower personally. I am told they visited Moret, went on to Grez, and took luncheon in the forest. They returned to dinner, and left the house, accompanied by Sir Gilbert and Lady Linton, to catch the last train to Paris just before I sat down to commence this letter. Sophia Kirby watched their departure through the bars of the window-shutter.

'I have nothing further at this moment to report—nothing of moment has occurred since I wrote a fortnight ago. My partner in London is, however, actively engaged in a new line of inquiry, which we confidently expect will result in a most important discovery.

'I am compelled to close my letter

hurriedly in view of the speedy return of Sir Gilbert and Lady Linton.

'Your respectful and obedient servant,

'E. Pierce.'

From the same, to Mr. Pierce, London.

'Valvins, Monday.

'Dear Pierce,

'Your demand for a written order empowering you to draw money out of the post-office, and accompanying letter, to hand. You are aware that every penny in the P. O. belongs to me, and that in the past I don't know many years you have done nothing but spend the money gained by my industry. I do not wish to rake up old grievances, and I am quite willing to accept your excuses and "make it up," as you propose. But, though we may be "the same flesh and blood," I have

no intention to let you participate in the
profits of my exertions unless you help me
to the best of your ability. As for your
threat to "drop a line to Sir Gilbert, and
so blow up the whole conspiracy," that is
a matter of perfect indifference to me,
for a reason that will appear here-
after.

'I do not wish to widen the breach
between us, Jo ; on the contrary, as you
will see by the enclosed notes for two
hundred francs—the Jew man in Fenchurch
Street will give you, less eighteenpence,
eight pounds for them, if you stick out
for the proper exchange. I wish to let
you see that I am most kindly disposed
towards you ; and I tell you this—that if
you only give me good proof of your
wish to serve me, I will listen favourably
to your notion of starting the United

Anglers' Punt Company or of taking the candle-factory.

'I want you, Jo, to find John Barton at once. This will not be very difficult, as I have discovered that he is guiltless of complicity in the murder of Lady L., has been thrown over by Sophia Kirby, and is in all probability dependent on his wits for a living.

'I am almost certain he is on the turf. S. K. is trying to find him. We must get at him first. She sent a letter to him at the Warden Hotel, Dover; but its contents show that she is doubtful of his getting it there.

'You will do well to go to the Warden and claim the letter. Not that it is of any value to us—I know the contents—*but because it would be valuable to him.* You had better advertise in the *Sporting Times*

and other turf-papers. If I knew the
addresses of these people, I would not
trouble you. Word it like this :

' "If John Barton wants to hear of a
good thing, write to ' double L., post office,
Dover.' "

' If there are any English sporting papers
published in Boulogne or Paris—I think
there must be—have the same advertisement inserted in them. You can take a
room somewhere in Dover, when you go
there to claim the letter at the Warden, and
wait for answers to the advertisements. It
is not unlikely that John Barton will
go to Dover himself. Be careful how you
manage him. If you find him, promise
him whatever you like, and, if possible, get
him to come to Fontainebleau with you.
Don't frighten him, or let him know more
than that you are acting for a lady. If

he answers by letter, send it to me at once.

'In either case communicate with me—by telegraph, if pressing.

'And now, Jo, that you may not go about this in a half-hearted reluctant fashion, I will let you into a secret—or part of it. I have discovered within the last week a fact which entirely alters the complexion of this affair. I give you my solemn word that I am working now for Lady L., and that, if I succeed, *she will bless the day that Mrs. Gower set us to destroy her happiness.*

'You see now how little I need care for your threat, and how, if you really sympathise with Lady L.—as you have professed—you are bound to help me to the utmost in your power. Write to me, enclosing copies of the advertisement,

and I will send you more money, and
continue the supply while you try to
aid me.

'Yours affectionately,

'E. PIERCE.

'P. S.—I need not enforce upon you the
necessity of absolute secrecy with regard to
our proceedings at the present time. Let
no one know what we are doing, nor even
suspect it by a careless word. It is not
probable that you will meet Mrs. Gower;
but, should such an accident occur, do not
suffer her to draw a single fact from you
relative to this affair. You know nothing
—the whole matter rests in the hands of
your partner at Fontainebleau, you can
say. Should she by any means get a
clue to the recent turn of events, my
plans will be upset, and all hopes of

rescuing Lady Linton from misery must
be abandoned.'

*   *   *   *   *

From Mr. Pierce, Dover, to Mrs. Pierce,
Fontainebleau.

'Sea View Cottage, Thursday.

'DEAR ELIZA,

'You've taken me out of my depth,
and where on earth you're going to land me
I don't know. However, I recognise the
wisdom of hanging on to you, and thank
you for the welcome notes. I am sorry to
see the money goes faster than I wish,
and must beg you to send me more before
long.

'Living is frightfully dear here—small
whisky, fourpence, and everything in

proportion. I have carried out your instructions to the letter, and enclose advertisements published in *Sporting Times*, *Field*, etc. I fetched the letter addressed to John Barton at the Warden and read it. It is all heathen Greek to me. But I have unbounded confidence in you, and am heartily glad to hear we are doing dirty work for clean people. I am certain a cheap bathing-company would do here—but of that more anon.

' Fish is scarcely to be obtained—the best being sent to London ; the remainder is sold in the town at a frightful price. I have been fairly lucky with a line fishing from a boat. A few boats started to supply the town with good fish ought to pay excellently. I am going to try a little bottom-fishing off Folkestone, and so adieu. Any information I may pick up relative to John Barton I will forward without delay.

'Yours most affectionately,

'Jos. Pierce.'

CHAPTER VIII

T was but a short period of happiness that came to little Lady Linton at this time—a stream of sunlight like that which sometimes succeeds a day of rain, irradiating for a moment the tear-washed face of Nature before the darkness of night veils it in deeper gloom.

Miss Drummond was not to be broken-in like a horse. If she submitted to Sir

Gilbert's guidance, it was simply because she saw the folly of running counter to him while he held the rein and the whip; meanwhile, she pondered the ways and means of getting the rein and whip into her own hands, and bringing Gilbert to submission in his turn.

Gertie saw nothing particular in the absence of Miss Drummond during the visit of Mr. Gower and his daughters. Possibly she was really unwell, possibly she was merely indisposed to meet visitors whose exuberant greeting indicated a character so entirely opposed to her own lethargic nature.

Gertie was heartily glad that she kept her room, for her presence would only have imposed constraint upon the girls, and spoilt her pleasure in their society.

How different it would have been, thought

she, if Gilbert had not come to an under-
standing with Miss Drummond ! Without
that she might have been openly insulted
before her own friends. She would certainly have felt anxious and ill at ease, and
they would have gone away with an im-
pression that she was unhappy.

Happily they had seen her at her best,
and found Gilbert, as he always was to her,
the handsomest, bravest, most courteous
gentleman in the world.

With some such reflections as these
Gertie fell asleep that night, after the
departure of her friends.

When she opened her eyes it was with a
confused notion that she had been listening
for some time to muffled voices and strange
sounds, such as she had heard in the vestibule on the night of Miss Drummond's
late return from Fontainebleau. She might

have been dreaming something of the kind. She found that Gilbert was not by her side. That did not alarm her.

He had been restless and unable to sleep soundly for some time—ever since Miss Drummond came to trouble them ; and frequently he rose in the night to seek sleep in the adjoining toilette-chamber, where an iron bedstead with a good hard mattress had been arranged for him at his direction.

The night was hot and close and very dark—after all, it might have been the roll of distant thunder which had disturbed her. She wondered what hour it was. She found her watch, and, touching the spring of the repeater, found it was after two.

Putting her watch back in the place from which she had taken it, she wondered if Gilbert were asleep.

'Happily he has no mental anxiety to keep him awake now,' she thought.

Then, sitting up in bed, she held her breath to catch the sound of his, if it were to be heard.

At that moment the sound of a laugh, speedily stifled, and the closing of a door fell upon her ear with startling clearness. The sounds came from the other end of the corridor, where Miss Drummond's rooms were situated.

For a moment Gertie was too astonished to reason upon what she had heard; then, fearful lest her dear husband should be disturbed, she slipped from the bed, intending to close the door opening on the corridor, which must certainly have come open for the sounds to be so distinct. No; the door was shut and fastened securely.

The sounds must have come through the door of the toilette-chamber. The door of connection with that room was wide open; she could see the stars through the window on the opposite side.

It was strange that he had not been woke. She would shut the door before he could be disturbed by a repetition of the noise.

Yes, the passage-door was open; it stood out in silhouette against the window as she entered the chamber. She had to pass Gilbert's bed to get to it. Moving cautiously forward, assuring herself of one step before venturing another, the silence struck her with sudden fear. She paused and stretched forth her right hand tentatively over the pillow, and then explored it with both. Gilbert was not there. She sat upon the bedside, unable to understand what it was that filled her with vague terror.

As she sat there in the darkness and silence of the night, her ear caught again that sound of laughter, deadened by the interposing door, and then the deep murmur of a man's voice. It was Gilbert's voice ; it was Miss Drummond's laugh.

Gertie started to her feet. In that moment of madness she had the intention of going to Miss Drummond's room and confronting the woman, with what purpose she knew not. It was the natural instinct of an outraged woman to give voice to the fury that raged within her.

But it was not the woman alone she should confront—her husband was there ; and at that thought she sank upon the bed, recoiling from the exposure of his infamy.

She felt that his shame was hers, and that it was a thing to hide from themselves and all the world. It seemed to her that she could never again look him in the face; that she must shut her eyes at the sight of him and shudder at his approach. But, apart from the sense of delicacy which made her shrink from the purpose which had a moment before possessed her, there was just sufficient reason glimmering over the heaving tumult of her mind to show her the impolicy of it. The shame would be for her in revealing the infidelity of her husband, the triumph for the woman who had succeeded in making him unfaithful. She had no sense of shame to touch—that creature, who made an open mock of innocence and faith, and delighted in the boast that she had never felt regret.

Gertrude was powerless to punish her,

and the woman knew it, and defiantly
showed that she knew it, by not even
closing the door to conceal her laughter.
Ah, was it not possible that she courted
discovery as a means of separating the wife
from the husband and getting him all to
herself? Why, that was most probable!
This supposition became a settled conviction from the moment it entered her mind.
When she could put her ideas into some
sort of consecutive order, Gertrude thought
thus :

‘ The woman came here with the express
intention of punishing me in revenge for
Gilbert's desertion, and of winning him
back to herself. She insulted me in the
very first hour of her coming. She made
herself the mistress of my house, ordered
my servants, directed my husband. She
made me ridiculous in his eyes—treating

me as a child and his toy. She missed no
opportunity to mortify me. She made love
to him shamelessly before my eyes. When
Gilbert saw how cruelly I suffered, he took
pity on me, and forbade her to continue
her systematic course of torture. Then she
prepared to strike a more deadly blow while
seeming to comply with his restrictions.
Oh, I have foreseen a new trouble ! I
have seen the brooding malice in her wicked
eyes as she lay there on the couch watching
me. And, now the blow is struck, what
help have I ?'

The cry came from her heart—' What
help have I ?' as she rose from the bed with
her hands clasped, staring into the darkness.

What could she do ? How could she
cope with that woman ? The admission of
her husband's infidelity must separate

them. She passed rapidly into her own room, with a vague feeling that she must hide her knowledge from Gilbert. She would go to bed again, and when he came she would pretend to be asleep. But with her hand upon the curtains she stopped. No, she could not deceive him. Good or bad, she could have no secret from him.

'God help me!' she moaned, sinking upon the chair by the window.

No, there could be no concealment. She could not live with him as if nothing had happened, even if she succeeded in hiding her knowledge. She could not meet that woman, exchange greetings with her, and bear a complacent countenance, knowing the connection that existed between her and Gilbert. She would rather suffer anything than that.

They must go away from each other, she and Gilbert, even if he offered to dismiss that woman. The shame would be too great for them to bear ; they could not live together with that fact even in their recollection ; they could not bear that degradation, remembering the purity of their former love.

She knew that men and their wives under similar conditions lived together, but that was because all love was gone between them. And she still loved her husband. There was no bitterness in her heart against him ; the woman was to blame, he to be pitied and wept for. Why, she knew not— did not seek to know ; only she felt it was so.

Oh, the happiness of the past gone for ever ! Would he not think of it with regret, and that aching sorrow at his heart which she felt ? And could he suffer so, and she not grieve for him ? It was the feeling of a mother for a child that has done wrong and suffers punishment. But it would be better for them both, better a thousand times, that they should go away from each other, suffer how they might, than that they should live together, hardening their hearts and growing callous to remorse, and slowly, surely ceasing to love each other in the pure sweet manner of old.

She would go away—no matter where, now that it was certain she must go—and find new friends. For it would be childlike to think of living all alone and dying of grief, as in old-fashioned romances. She must get over it somehow ; and that could only be done by a great effort not to give way to sentiment too much, and by grasping every chance of strengthening her heart and mind.

She would try to find friends—two or three, not more. Not granny nor the girls — oh no! she hoped they would never hear about Gilbert! Perhaps she would go to Neufbourg, or some remote place where no one could know that she had been married, and had lost her husband. But this suggested a new calamity to her mind.

Her child—their child! the new being whose coming had been the centre of her happy dreams by day and night— the fruit of their dear love—the link which was to bind her husband yet more closely to her—the soul that they were to cherish together, to train up graciously, and mould to the form most lovable and good!

'Oh, Gilbert, Gilbert! have you never

thought of that ?' she murmured; and then of a sudden her heart broke in sobs, and the tears sprang from her eyes.

This outburst of grief was not of long duration. She stanched the tears and set herself to think with desperate resolution—set herself to think collectedly, with the sobs yet shaking her body and the tears slowly streaming from her eyes, wipe them how she might.

It was not for herself she had to think now—it was for her child—for Gilbert's child. The welfare of that hapless creature was of far more importance than her happiness. She must find out what it was her duty to do, what sacrifice she could make for the sake of her unborn child.

Her head grew giddy and ached with

the effort she made to compose her thoughts and bring them into reasonable form. She thought that she might be able to grow calm if she walked about the room instead of sitting still ; and she rose from her chair and groped her way forward in the darkness.

At that moment Gilbert entered the room with noiseless step, and, seeing her ghostly figure in the pale light of the stars, knew what had happened.

CHAPTER IX.

A MAN'S TEARS.

'GERTIE!' he said, in a low tone, speaking that she might not be frightened by discovering him unwarned.

'I am here, dear,' she answered, in faltering tones.

He had come, and she was unprepared. She was helpless, and stood trembling and weak; wondering simply if she ought to have called him 'dear' if they were to go away from one another.

He came to her side, and putting his hand upon her shoulder, felt her shivering beneath his touch.

'Better get into bed, my child,' he said gently.

'No, no; I cannot lie down. There is too much to think about,' she replied, trembling violently.

He led her forward without speaking, and obliged her to sit on the bed; then he groped about in search of a covering for her, remembered his dressing - gown, and fetched it and put it on her shoulders, found a pair of slippers and put them on her feet, while she sobbed in bewilderment and uncertainty.

It seemed to her that he ought to be altered somehow; yet here he was the same thoughtful tender man, going about

noiselessly, and seeking practical comfort
for her.

She had always loved him so dearly,
believed in him so thoroughly, regarded
him so clearly as an absolutely good
and perfect husband, that she could not
all of a sudden cease to love and respect
and honour him.

Weakly she yearned, and, knowing she
was weak, yet yearned for a restoration
of that perfect love that had existed, if
only for one moment, that she might
draw him to her and kiss him in grati-
tude for putting his dressing-gown about
her.

It was so contrary to all she had ever
thought or expected that she could not
realize his guilt. Theoretically she saw
that the love between them must be at

an end; but practically she loved him still.

He sat down on the bed beside her, and it seemed quite natural that he should put his arm round her; but, oh, it was terrible to be unable to clasp the hand that touched her waist! And she must never, never kiss him again! Had she lost him for ever?

Her heart was wrung between conflicting emotions for a moment; and then, giving way to the impulse of her nature, she turned towards him, flung her arms about his neck, and burst into tears.

He alone knew what he suffered as he sat there, powerless to soothe the distracted wife, whose heart-breaking sobs sounded in his ear as they convulsed the tender body under his hand.

He took a handkerchief from his pocket

and pressed it against the cheek that lay upward from his breast.

'Yes, dear, yes,' she said, accepting this act as a hint, and drawing herself up ; 'I shall be calm directly.' She took the handkerchief, and, after a long quivering sob, said, with an air of buoyant resolution, 'Now we will talk about it, and settle what is to be done!'

'No hurry, Gertie.'

'Oh, yes, yes! We must think it out now. I was trying to think it out alone when you came. It will be easier with you to help me.'

'Well, sweetheart?'

'Oh, you mustn't call me that! I know —I know all.'

'So I supposed. You overheard all—eh?'

'Oh, Gilbert! You don't think I would listen at a door, do you?'

' How could you know without ?'

' I found your door open—I heard your voice—I heard that horrid creature laugh.'

' Is that all ?' he said, not in a tone of inquiry, but with a sigh of regret. ' I hoped it was all over,' he added absently.

She listened in astonishment. What did he mean by hoping it was all over? Had she not heard enough to separate them ?

Did he wish that she had obtained more conclusive evidence, that any temporization might be impossible, or—and she clutched at the possibility with a desperate hope of escape—had she rashly jumped at a wrong conclusion and condemned him upon insufficient evidence? Did he hope that she had discovered a fact that would allay her suspicions and put an end to the cruel doubts by which he suffered in part with her.

But, while she waited in feverish suspense, he spoke, and his words banished hope from her heart.

' After what you have heard,' he said, ' it would be an absurdity to remind you that you promised to have faith in me, and to ask you to trust me in spite of these damning proofs. You are no longer a child, and you never were a fool.'

' I am not a child, Gilbert,' she replied ; ' but I have faith in you; and if you tell me that my suspicions are all wrong and groundless, I will—I——' she hesitated, seeing how hard it would be to reconcile his fidelity to her with the circumstances ; and then, determined to set his word above her own reason, she added, in a low earnest tone—' I *will* believe you.'

He did not reply for some time. At length he said:

'I don't see how that's possible, Gertie. Or, if it is possible to strain credulity so far this time, it might not be the next, and all this misery would be repeated. Come, tell me what you thought when you heard our voices out there.'

'I thought I could never look you in the face again—that we never could approach each other without a sort of horror of each other. And then it would kill all the tender and good feelings in us to live together with that on our minds.'

'But you don't seem to have much horror just now?' he said, almost playfully, touching the hand that clung to his arm.

'No, no! I cannot understand myself. You are so unchanged, so calm and kind,

so exactly like your old self, the man I
have worshipped and loved above all the
world, that somehow I can't realize that
you have done wrong and are changed.'

'The strongest love needs time to
mature; detestation may be the stronger
for not coming in a moment. And I don't
see how you can stand a continuation of
this kind of thing without eventually hating
me. That's the devil of it!' He spoke
with bitter impatience, was silent a moment, then continued in a calmer tone, 'Go
on, Gertie; let me know what you thought
of doing.'

'I thought that it would be better to go
away at once, Gilbert,' she said, trembling.

He did not reply.

'Go right away—separate, perhaps for—
for ever,' she sobbed.

He said nothing to show that he was

at all surprised ; rather his silence led her to suppose that he had calculated upon such a possibility.

A terrible fear that he would be content to let her go away flashed upon her ; but she shut her eyes to it ; she would not think him so heartless and cruel ; it was treason to do so. And she stifled her sobs and hurried on, lest he might say something to verify her greatest fear.

'Then, dear, I saw how wrong that would be,' she said, 'and that we had something more to consider than our own feelings.'

He turned to her with an exclamation of inquiry.

'We have to think of the future,' she continued—'of our little one.'

'Good God !' he murmured in an undertone.

'I knew you had not thought of that as I have. It is natural I should think of it a great deal. What should I do, dear, if we were apart—for you would not take my child from me, would you ?'

' Heaven forbid !'

' And how terrible it would be for you to have a child and yet be a stranger to it ! Think of that !'

' I am thinking how terrible it would be for you.'

' And for him—if a son is born to us. How should I answer his first questions ? I could not tell a lie to him, and I—oh, I could not tell him the truth ! And people would pity him, and he must think that some great wrong had been done to separate us. And how could I—— I could never mention your name to him, never teach him to love and honour you; scarcely could I dare to tell him what honour and truth are, with the shadow of dishonour and infidelity hanging over me. And so I came to see that we could not part. And that will not be so hard as it seems at first sight, for in our hearts we love each other still. You do not love that—that——'

'Love her!' he cried, with a contemptuous laugh.

'If you have done wrong, it is from want of thought. I can make allowances for men who are tempted. She has told me what to expect, and, though I would not think it of you, I—I think I can forgive, and grow more like a woman of the world. I think I could do anything for the sake of our child, Gilbert.'

'It will be strange if I can't do something also,' he said. 'It won't do to part—that's impossible—more impossible than ever. Thank God, you've a strong heart, Gertie — the strongest and best in this world, I do believe! Come, dear, we've had our talk out, and you'll have need yet of all your strength; so get to bed again and sleep, if you can, to meet to-morrow's struggle bravely. I'll go and get a breath of fresh air outside as soon as I see you in a fair way to fall asleep.'

Gertie obeyed instinctively. And when she had slipped into bed he arranged her pillow, drew the curtains so that the morning light should not wake her, and, bending down, kissed her twice, saying, in his tenderest, gentlest manner :

'A little patience, sweetheart!'

She held his face to hers and would have spoken, but that wonder and pity took away the power, for she found that his cheek was wet.

Once before, and only once, she had found traces of tears on his face; and now, as then, it stirred her heart with profound emotion to know that a man so great and strong as Gilbert could give way to grief like a weak woman.

And, oh, the joy that was mingled with her compassion and wonder to find that he grieved! If he had shown signs of guilt and made her believe that he had done wrong, she must have forgiven him and loved him more than ever now, finding him in sorrow.

CHAPTER X.

MISS DRUMMOND'S NEW TACTICS.

SHE did not fall asleep for a long while after he left her. Her thoughts were too distinct to permit of drowsiness.

As the excitement passed away and her mind grew more tranquil, she obtained a clearer perception of her position and of the difficulties which faced her.

She had settled as a necessary condition of her staying with her husband that he should send Miss Drummond out of the house. But he had not mentioned a word of her going.

He had accepted the fact that his wife could not leave, but he had given her the very vaguest encouragement to think that her existence would be made more endurable.

He had even hinted that what had occurred might occur again. Could she endure that?

She had talked of becoming a woman of the world, and of the necessity of palliating the society-faults of a husband. But she had spoken of these things in a moment of hopefulness, as one talks bravely of fighting against odds when there is no sign of a battle.

Calm reflection, however, brought her one cold comfort, and that was that her

jealousy had made her wrongly suspi-
cious. Gilbert had not been unfaithful
to her.

Nothing but the recklessness of a man
perfectly vile or perfectly mad would
account for an intrigue being carried out
with such an utter disregard to discovery.
Gilbert was neither vile nor mad.

Again, could any man after the discovery
of his iniquity have behaved as Gilbert
behaved? Certainly not.

She did not know exactly how guilty
persons would act, but she felt quite
confident that they would not act in
that way.

He had not refuted the implied charge
against him because the charge was con-
temptible, or because a denial of that would
have involved a disclosure of something
else which he did not wish to make. It

was no secret that something was concealed from her.

While she was happy she had been content to leave the mystery unsolved. Her faith in Gilbert was so complete that she had not questioned for a moment the wisdom and justice of his reticence. It was manly, in her opinion, to be silent on a subject which he deemed not fit for her to know. Only women betray their secrets.

But now that she was no longer happy, and that her faith had received a rude shock, she began to consider what the secret was which ranked before her peace and happiness.

And, though she imagined many wild and improbable things, she never once thought that her husband and Miss Drummond shared the guilt of Lady

Linton's murder between them. Gilbert had not yet sunk low enough in her esteem for that.

It was not until her mind was confused with conflicting conjectures, and the sound of the servants moving about the house fell upon her ears, that she fell asleep.

When Pierce came at the regular hour and tapped at the door, she woke, with a confused remembrance of the night's events, a sense of weariness, and a desire to sleep again and forget.

Her heart sickened at the thought of meeting Miss Drummond, and for a moment she thought of escaping the ordeal by pleading indisposition; but she was stung by the reflection that the woman would suspect what had happened and would exult in her prostration; and she thereupon resolved to go down in the

ordinary way and face her courageously—
just as if she knew nothing—should that be
possible.

There was a lurking jealousy in her
heart, despite the conclusion she had drawn
of Gilbert's innocence. She was painfully
conscious that she had been unjust to her
husband; and, remembering his grief, she
accused herself of being a trouble rather
than a comfort to him.

Then she hurried through her toilette,
that she might go down to him and make
atonement as best she could.

Leaving her room, she met a chamber-
maid coming from Miss Drummond's room.
A rank nauseous odour of stale eau de
Cologne pervaded the corridor; the maid
carried a liqueur-set on a tray in her right
hand, and with her left held up the corners
of her apron.

Lady Linton stopped, with an inquiring glance; the maid opened her lap and exposed the fragments of a large flacon, held together in part by the label of 'Jean Marie Farina,' with that complacent smile which servants all the world over wear in presence of an accident.

'You have had an accident, Marie?'

'No, madam. I found the pieces upon the floor in mademoiselle's room.'

'Ah, Miss Drummond has left her room?'

'She descended an hour ago, madam.'

This was contrary to Miss Drummond's habit. Gertie went down, imagining new evils.

She passed into the library; neither Gilbert nor Miss Drummond was there. On her way to the salon she met Pierce.

'Sir Gilbert is in the salon?' she said inquiringly.

'No, madam; I have not seen Sir Gilbert this morning.'

'Miss Drummond?'

'Miss Drummond went out half an hour ago.'

Gertie passed through the salon and out under the veranda, trying to think that there was nothing peculiar in the absence of 'that woman' and her husband. It was a charming morning; the garden with the meadow beyond, the forest, and the glimpse of shining river, had never looked more beautiful. Yet she saw nothing there that brightened her spirits or chased away for one moment the gloomy sense of monotony that oppressed her.

The goat with her young in the meadow,

catching sight of her, ran round in a circle at the end of the tether, bringing herself up with a jerk occasionally, and bleating to be set free as usual; but Gertie did not seem to hear or see anything. She turned her back upon the garden with a feeling of weakness, and seated herself in the darkest corner of the salon to indulge in morbid reflection.

At another time she would have been concerned only for Gilbert; his long absence would have filled her heart with endearing solicitude; she would have gone to the farthest corner of the meadow to look along the road and see if he were in sight. Now she did nothing of the kind. She sat and thought of herself, saying again and again that she was unreasonable and wrong, and yet having no power to be reasonable and right.

She had promised him to have patience, she had come to a just conclusion that he was guiltless; it was the most improbable thing in the world that he had made an appointment to meet Miss Drummond this morning.

All this Gertie knew without feeling any better for the knowledge. Reason is powerless against an attack of jealousy, as against any other form of madness.

At the first sound of a voice Gertie started from her seat, and went out on the terrace, saying to herself that the creature should have no cause to think she was jealous of her.

Contrary to her expectation, Miss Drummond was alone; but that did not alleviate Gertie's suspicions. Of course the horrid thing would pretend she had not gone out to meet Gilbert, she said to herself.

Miss Drummond was coming down the
path from the wood; she held a piece of
meadow-sweet in her hand—she professed
to hate wild flowers.

She was humming an air as she came
along, and, with her head tilted a little
back, she scanned Gertie with impudent
assurance through her pince-nez.

Gertie tried to look indifferent, her heart
beating painfully and an uncontrollable
quivering in her lips. A very simple
student of character would have detected
her agitation.

'Baby not quite well this morning?'
asked Miss Drummond, with mocking
sympathy, as she drew near. 'You should
try the effect of early rising and fresh air.
I had no idea they could be so pleasant.
Had a quite charming ramble—all alone—
over the hills there. What's the name of

this charming flower? It reminds me of some hot-house thing I have seen somewhere.'

'It is spirea, and it generally grows beside the river.'

'Odd I should have found it on the hill then, isn't it? Bertie down yet?'

Gertrude wished to say something scathing with regard to the sprig of spirea; but, for people not naturally ill-tempered, it is the most difficult thing possible to be cleverly sarcastic at a moment's notice; and she failed dismally in the attempt. Her words got mixed; she stuttered painfully. Miss Drummond assisted her.

'I know what you would say, Baby,' she said, tapping her playfully with her spray, and smiling with as much good-humour as the unpleasant lines of her lips

permitted. ' You would say that the only
thing odd about my finding it on a hill is
that I found it without assistance. Naughty
—very naughty indeed !'

And, with a final tap, she passed into
the salon, her retroussé nose in the air, and
her full pendulous lips parted and drawn
back at the angles in the nearest resem-
blance to an expression of amiability she
could command.

A minute later Gilbert entered the
meadow by the wicket opening upon the
road by the river.

Of course he came that way ; but it was
rather indiscreet to arrive so speedily after
Miss Drummond, thought Gertie; then she
said to herself that she would not go to
meet him, but stay where she stood, and
greet him with the cold formality of a
self-possessed woman of the world—such a

woman as he was making her, and as she must become in time.

She would not even move from the trellis that concealed her from him; that would show how indifferent she felt.

He came along the path with his face to her. He saw a part of her skirt, and knew she was there.

He made fully a dozen paces from the wicket, the skirt not moving, and then— she stepped from the terrace, sped swiftly across the lawn, and, with distraction in her face and gesture, threw herself into his arms.

There was an aperture in the hedge, with a seat that commanded a view of the river. In there one was screened from observation.

He led her to it and made her sit down by his side, for he saw Miss Drummond standing under the veranda by the entrance to the salon.

'Oh, you mustn't kiss me, you mustn't hold me!' she murmured, with her face against his breast; 'I don't deserve it! I am a wicked girl, dear, wicked and cruel. I saw you the moment you came in by the gate; but I wouldn't come to you, and I tried to harden my heart and think the hardest, cruellest things I could of you; and then I saw your dear face looking so tired and careworn, and I couldn't be hard any longer, and I was compelled to give in; but it wasn't from any generous motive, only just because I couldn't help it. Oh, you don't know how unjust and selfish I have been, not once thinking of what you have to bear, but only of my own troubles! And I felt quite willing to give you pain.'

'Why?' he asked.

'Because she went out to meet you, and came back with a piece of meadow-sweet in her hand, and tried to make me believe that you had given it to her. And I believed her and my own evil suspicions, rather then put faith in you. Yet somehow, underneath all, I knew that I was wrong, and that she was misleading me intentionally, and I knew that she had not met you, and that you do not love her at all.'

He answered her with a troubled laugh. It was the only denial he gave to her suspicions; but for the time it was enough.

CHAPTER XI.

LADY LINTON'S TROUBLES REACH A CLIMAX.

HE whole of that day and the next, Gertie was proof against the insidious attacks of her enemy; and with all a bad woman's subtle cunning, Miss Drummond endeavoured to shake her faith in Gilbert and provoke her jealousy.

When he was reading, she looked over his shoulder, resting her hands on the back of his chair, and bringing her face so near his that her hair touched his ; a flower he brought in with the intention of giving to his wife, she stole and hid in her bosom.

She begged him to pass things, and needlessly touched his hand ; she fixed her eyes upon him, and dropped hers in confusion when she succeeded in attracting his attention; she found pretexts to follow him wherever he went; she unfolded and read mysterious scraps of paper covered with a bold handwriting that looked like his.

She pretended, when Gertie entered the room, to be taken by surprise, controlling a smile, throwing a fan up before her face, stifling an exclamation, removing herself hastily from Gilbert—and all this in a covert manner which might lead Gertie to suppose that she had found out by her own shrewd observation that which was intended to be seen by her.

Gertie had Gilbert's support. He would not leave her. A word or a look from him undid all the mischief made by Miss Drummond. He redoubled his attentions, and lost no chance of giving her a proof of his love.

Gertie felt ashamed, seeing the motive which underlay his constant care. She felt so confident of her strength, now that her first feebleness was past, that she almost wished he would leave her to fight the enemy alone. But Gilbert knew that the heart that had once yielded to jealousy was not safe from another seizure; and his anxiety gave him no rest.

It was a relief when, on the third day, Miss Drummond's convenient headache confined her to her room. Gertie insisted upon her husband going for a walk; and he, after half an hour's reflection, went.

An hour afterwards, Miss Drummond appeared with her thumb and finger on her brows. She really thought she must go and have some advice about her head, which was quite too troublesome; and if Gertie had no use for the phaeton—— Gertie, only too glad to get her out of the house, was most happy to lend her the phaeton, and found the cards of several doctors which had been left soon after their arrival.

While the carriage was being prepared, Miss Drummond would write a little note she wished to post at Fontainebleau, and went into the library for that purpose.

At three o'clock she left the house; at half-past four Gertie heard wheels on the drive. A little later, Pierce entered to learn at what hour madam would dine.

'That will depend on Sir Gilbert's return. Come to me in an hour. That was the phaeton I heard, with Miss Drummond, I suppose?'

'The phaeton, madam, but not Miss Drummond.'

Gertie ceased stitching, and lifted her head in surprise.

'Without Miss Drummond!' she exclaimed. 'Has Louis brought any message for me?'

'No, madam. I considered it my duty to ask him if he had a message for madam. He replied that Miss Drummond had given him a note for Sir Gilbert, which he had delivered — having overtaken him on his return from the station.'

'The station! I understood that—

Miss Drummond did not go on to the town ?'

'No, madam. Has madam any further requirements ?'

'You can go.'

Gertie mused for a few minutes, then returned to her work, stitching thought-fully.

At six o'clock Pierce brought a telegram to her. She hastily took the slip of blue paper from the envelope and read:

> '*From*
> 'M. GILBERT LINTON,
> 'Melun.

'I may be unable to leave here until to-morrow. If I can return before, I shall. In either case, be sure that my stay is unavoidable.'

'There is no return message,' said Gertie brightly.

She had determined to give her husband a convincing proof of her trust in him, and she faced the possibility of Miss Drummond being at Melun with her husband bravely. It might be a matter of business—something to do with the house Miss Drummond was seeking, perhaps. At any rate, she would not let the accidental discovery that Miss Drummond had gone to the station, after stating her intention of going to the town, weigh upon her mind, any more than the fact that Gilbert had received a letter from her before going to Melun.

She dined alone; it was infinitely pleasanter than dining with Miss Drummond—Gilbert being unavoidably detained at Melun—would have been. She dispensed with nothing because of her being alone, and sipped her coffee under the veranda as if Gilbert had been there; then, in bethinking herself how she might pass the evening pleasantly, she resolved to write a long letter to granny.

She had the reading-lamp lit and taken into the library; then she shut herself in, and, sitting down at the table, opened the writing-case which Gilbert had bought in Paris for her.

Some one had been writing in it; there, on the white blotting-paper, was the copy of a great irregular scrawl done with a quill-pen. It was not Gilbert's writing; it was certainly not her own. Suddenly she remembered that Miss Drummond had written a note before going out.

Ah, it was sacrilege for that creature to use the present which Gilbert had given her! She tore the page out of it without hesitating a moment, and crushed it in her

hand. Suddenly she stopped, as if spell-
bound. In crumpling the paper she
exposed the back of it; the heavy writing
had stained through the flimsy substance;
one word caught her eye. She stood for a
moment motionless with the paper in her
hand, and the one word before her eyes.
Then she yielded to the temptation,
unfolded the paper, and read :

'Thanks—a thousand times thanks for
your dear note. How kind of Baby! I
shall be there, of course. But why Melun?
Why not—— But I must have patience.

'Ever

'Your Own.'

*　　　*　　　*　　　*　　　*

Gilbert came home after midnight. He
saw through the persiennes light in the

library. Gertie opened the door to him. There was no light in the vestibule. She looked like a spectre against the dark background; her hand was damp and icy cold.

She stood there looking beyond him, as if expecting to find him accompanied by some one.

'No, there is no one there,' he said. 'I am quite alone. What is the matter, Gertie?'

She closed the door without speaking, and, by the hand he still held in his, led him silently into the library. Her eyes were red and swollen; they heightened the ghastly pallor of her cheeks. Her silence and her appearance frightened him.

She led him to the table, and put the sheet of paper in his hand. He glanced at the paper, then at her, and then again at the paper.

'What is this?' he asked, in a tone of perplexity, having deciphered the blotted words.

'A copy of the letter Louis gave you before you went to Melun, I suppose,' she said, speaking with violent agitation.

He took her by the arms and compelled her to sit in the big chair.

'Are any of the servants up?' he asked.

'I don't know,' she said vacantly.

He touched the bell, and, standing by it for a moment, turned the blotting-paper over, glanced at the open writing-case on the table, and understood what had happened. That model servant Pierce responded promptly.

'Make me some tea, and bring it in here,' he said.

Then, as Pierce withdrew, he came to Gertie's side, and, half seating himself upon the arm of her chair, rested his elbow on the back of it, and let his hand fall lightly on his wife's head.

At his touch she put her hands up to her face and burst into tears. He suffered her to weep, almost envying her that relief to an overburdened heart. Meanwhile, he grappled again with the vexed question— what was to be done?

His left hand had slid into his pocket. He felt there the letter that Louis had given him. He remembered its contents word for word.

'I cannot endure this monotony. I am going to Melun. You had better come to take care of me.'

Those were the words of which Gertie
fancied she had the copy. Should he put
the letter before his wife? Should he show
her how unnecessary the letter was if he
had previously appointed to meet Miss
Drummond at Melun, how unlikely that
he should return to get her reply if he
intended going to Melun, how improbable
that any woman in her senses would
have blotted such a letter on an open
pad, and left the evidence for anyone to
read?

Should he, in short, show her how weak
she had been to step so readily into such
a very palpable snare as that which this
woman had laid for her? He foresaw
pretty clearly what would happen if he
did do so.

Gertie would be overwhelmed with shame
and contrition once more, she would torture

herself with reproaches, she would oppose
herself to fresh dangers in order to prove
her resolution to overcome them, and would
inevitably refuse to escape the persecutions
of Miss Drummond by flight, as being
an ignominious concession to her own
weakness.

The only prospect of obtaining peace
and happiness lay in flight; he was only
waiting for a favourable opportunity. To
delay their flight was simply to expose
this devoted, loving, unreasonable little wife
to just such another complication.

As these reflections came to his mind, he
sat looking down with mournful love at
Gertie's bowed head, passing his fingers
gently over the shining ripples of her hair
with pathetic purposelessness.

Gertie ceased to cry as the paroxysm of
grief passed away; but her sobs continued,

like the sound of drops falling from the trees when the shower is over.

Gilbert rose and went to the door, when his attentive ear caught the approach of Pierce's steps on the vestibule. He took the tray from her hand, and told her, in a low voice, that he might want her later on.

He poured out a cup of tea, sweetened it and put it before Gertie; then, as he helped himself, he said:

'Drink that, Gertie, and when we feel a little more like ourselves we'll talk this thing out reasonably, and have done with it once for all.'

Gertie, after giving her poor eyes a final rub, gulped down a little tea, and stole a furtive glance at her husband. He had gone to the sideboard, and was slowly filling his pipe.

Oh, he could not behave in that manner if he were guilty! He wasn't heartless. No man in the world was so sympathetic as he.

Already her mind began to waver, and a dim presentiment that she should presently find herself to blame made itself felt.

Gilbert lit his pipe over the lamp, then turned it down quite low, emptied his cup, and seated himself once more on the arm of Gertie's chair; only now he kept his hands in his pockets.

'Of course, Gertie,' he said, in his firm, yet not ungentle tone, 'you made up your mind what must follow, before you determined to show me that—that message of Miss Drummond's.'

The admission that it was a message

strengthened Gertie in the bitter resolve
she had taken.

'I could have no self-respect if I ignored
it, Gilbert,' she said.

'Of course not.'

'And without self-respect, I—I couldn't
hope to have your respect?'

'I suppose that's about what it would
come to.'

'And I don't think I could live without
that,' she said, with a sob.

Gilbert's pipe trembled in his lips. He
said nothing.

'And—and, feeling that we could not
go on in this way,' she continued, after
a pause, 'I thought that the sooner it
ended the better it would be for you and
me.'

'That is true, Gertie.'

'But it is such a terrible thing for a husband and wife to part, especially——'

She stopped—the words seeming to choke her—and held her lip between her teeth while her trembling fingers tightened on the hem of his coat, with which they had been toying.

'Especially,' she continued, with an effort—'if they—they have loved as—as we have——'

She broke down in a fluttering sob and a little moan, and her hands were raised again to cover her face.

Gilbert took the pipe from his mouth and slipped it into his pocket, and drew a long silent sigh, looking down, as through a mist, at his grief-stricken, suffering wife.

'That I thought,' she pursued, overcoming her weakness with a desperate

shake of her head, 'for my sake, and
for our child's, you would do something
to avoid such a — such a misfortune,
dear.'

'What do you wish me to do, Gertie?
I want to know what that something
is.'

'I think—if that woman were away,' she
faltered—'if you were removed from the
constant temptation she sets before you,
that everything would come right again,
dear—almost.'

'Yes.'

'And so if you would—would send her
away, Gilbert——'

She stopped, and waited for his reply—
not daring to look up at him.

'But suppose she won't go ; suppose I
can't send her away——'

'Then I see no help for it,' she said

despairingly ; ' I must go ! But, Gilbert,
my husband—can't you send her away ?'
She raised her tear-dimmed eyes to his
imploringly, and lifted up her hands.

For a moment he hesitated, then, taking
her hand, he said :

' I can't, Gertie. You must go !'

She snatched her hand from his with
passionate anger, and rose to her feet, looking at him with contempt, her pride lending
her strength.

' You prefer that creature to me ?' she
asked.

' I have never given you cause to think
so,' he answered.

' Not when you bid me leave my own
house, that she may stay ?'

' There is a reason for my refusing to
send her away, which I cannot explain to
you.'

'Why not? Can you tell me anything more degrading to yourself, more insulting to me, than that which you have calmly told me—that of us two that woman must stay, and I must go?'

'I think there is.'

He did not wish to carry the explanation farther. He did not wish to excuse himself.

He was so grateful to think that her pride, which it wrung his heart to wound, would help her to bear up a little longer against her troubles. It needed but a tender word—a warm look, even—to melt her heart.

He had risen from the arm of the chair when she rose, and they had stood face to face; he turned away, lest she should discover in his face the woe he felt in her unhappiness, the yearning in his heart to take her in his arms and soothe her tortured spirit.

'You have told me I must go,' she said bitterly; 'you have only to tell me when!'

He pulled a note-book from his pocket, and turned to a list of trains written there.

'There's a train at 2.40,' he said; then, looking at his watch, he added, '1.30—we could just do it.'

'We!' she exclaimed, as he went to the bell.

'You don't think I'm quite such a brute as to send you off in the dead of the night alone, do you, Gertie?' he asked, with a solemnity which to anyone but those two would have seemed comic.

'Wake Louis at once,' he said, addressing

Pierce as she opened the library-door. 'Tell him the brougham must be at the door in twenty-five minutes ; and then come back to me here.'

CHAPTER XII.

CORRESPONDENCE.

From Mr. Pierce, Dover, to Mrs. Pierce.
Fontainebleau.

'Dover, *Aug.* 12.

'MY DEAR ELIZA,

'One line to let you know that I have succeeded in finding John Barton's friend, if it isn't John Barton himself. He's a scarey bird; and it takes unlimited Irish to get a word out of him. He wishes to know—always on behalf of his friend—what the good thing is.

'Please let me know at once what I'm to do with him. We are now off to an adjacent beershop to play a game of bagatelle.

'Yours, in haste, affectionately,

'Jos. Pierce.'

From Mrs. Gower, London, to Mrs. Pierce, Fontainebleau.

'Mrs. Gauntly Gower regrets that the visit of Mr. Gower to Sir Gilbert Linton's was not productive of more satisfactory results, and feels justified in stating that recent communications from E. Pierce have been less assuring than formerly.

'Mrs. Gauntly G. is of opinion that further measures should be taken without delay for bringing the business to a climax, and sees no reason why she herself should not be confronted with Sophia Kirby. She remembers her with sufficient distinctness to swear to her identity, and this would at once serve to bring the culprits within the grasp of the law.

'If E. Pierce will so arrange affairs as to permit of Mrs. Gauntly Gower's being introduced privately into Sir G. Linton's house, Mrs. Gauntly G. will undertake the journey without delay.

' Cheque to follow.

'Gauntly House, *Aug.* 12, 188—.'

From Mrs. E. Pierce, Fontainebleau, to Mr. Pierce, Dover.

'Valvins, *Aug.* 14.

" DEAR PIERCE,

' I shall in all likelihood be at Dover to-morrow or the day after. Stay in Dover. Pretend to be ill and keep in bed ; get J. B.

to stay with you. Spend what you please upon liquor for that purpose, or ask him to play you at cards, and lose.

'If I find him with you when I arrive it will be all right. Things couldn't be going better for you, me, and the right party.

' Affectionately,

' E. PIERCE.

' P.S.—Do not let J. B. know that you expect to see me.'

From the same to Mrs. Gower, London.

'Valvins, *Aug.* 14.

' DEAR MADAM,

' Your note of the 12th inst. to hand. If we had considered your services necessary to the success of our inquiry, we should not have hesitated in soliciting them. If, on the other hand, we did not feel ourselves capable of conducting our business without the advice of our clients, we should not have undertaken this investigation.

'We hold ourselves free at all times to limit our communications within those bounds which we consider prudent.

'Yours respectfully,

'E. PIERCE.

'P.S.—Be good enough to address future correspondence to "E. Pierce, Post-Office, Dover."'

From Mrs. Gower, London, to Mrs. Pierce, Dover.

'Mrs. Gauntly Gower sincerely regrets that the intention of her last note was misconstrued.

' She is too sensible of the ability with which Messrs. Pierce and Pierce have conducted the present investigation to place her own views above theirs, or to wish to interfere with their arrangements.

' Mrs. Gauntly Gower merely wished to intimate that she should be happy to render any assistance in her power, and that she should be grateful for any information which Messrs. P. and P. might feel themselves justified in giving with regard to the progress of their inquiry, especially as relates to the most recent events, and encloses cheque in payment of services to end of present month.

' Gauntly House, *Aug.* 16, 188—.'

*From Mrs. Pierce, Dover, to Mrs. Gourer,
London.*

'Dover, *Aug.* 17.

'Dear Madam,

'Your note of the 16th inst., in-
closing cheque, to hand. I return receipt,
with thanks, and have great pleasure in
complying with your request for information. I have already informed you of the
line of conduct taken by Sophia Kirby
upon her arrival at Valvins, and of her
insulting behaviour towards Lady Linton.
That line of conduct Sir Gilbert tolerated
until he perceived that the constant strain
was telling severely upon Lady Linton's
health.

'He then in a private interview with
S. K. intimated that she must leave the
house at once or treat his wife with proper
consideration, and signified that he would

rather face the consequences of a complete exposure than suffer Lady L. to endure a system of persecution which was more insupportable than her knowledge of his offence.

'S. K., seeing the inadvisability of a rupture by which she would be the greatest sufferer, immediately changed her tactics. She ceased to openly insult Lady L., and abandoned the tone of insolent authority she had assumed.

'But she proceeded in a covert manner to excite Lady L.'s jealousy, with a view to producing a misunderstanding between her and her husband, and succeeded so well that, on the night of Aug. 11, Lady L., provoked to a state of frenzy, told Sir G. that she would no longer stay in the house with "Miss Drummond," and that he must choose between his wife and her.

S. K. was at this time absent from the house.

'Sir G., with a motive which I will presently explain, replied that he could not send "Miss Drummond" away, and that she, his wife, must go. He ordered the carriage to be brought at once, and bade me pack up whatever would be needful to Lady L. for three or four days.

'While he gave these orders Lady L. sat in a helpless state of bewilderment, as if all power to think or to act had gone from her mind. I brought the things I had packed in Sir G.'s valise, and asked if I were to accompany Lady L.

'"No," he replied; "but you will prepare to follow her ladyship to-morrow. You will stay here. If Miss Drummond arrives before I return, tell her I expect to arrive about mid-day to-morrow."

'He then desired his wife to put on her bonnet and mantle. The unhappy lady obeyed without a word, but, without my support, I feel sure she must have fallen upon the stairs, her agitation was so great. She took her husband's portrait from a drawer, but nothing else, and we then went down to the hall.

'Sir Gilbert was standing by the open door. The carriage had just arrived. She paused a moment, and then, leaving me, hurried into the drawing-room. I heard a key turn, and knew what she had gone for. In her work-table she kept the baby's things she had been making during the last few weeks. Sir Gilbert saw her go in, but he did not follow. He went out and waited in the dark.

'Lady L. was some time gone; but, when I moved towards the door, she came out with her head bent down and her arms folded over her breast. A little white cuff protruded from the opening in her mantle. She covered it with her hands, and I saw the tears splash down upon her hand. She had not heard Sir Gilbert say I was to follow, evidently, for, as I stood back after helping her into the brougham, she said in a choked voice:

· "Thank you, Pierce. Good-bye!"

'Sir Gilbert stepped into the carriage, after telling the driver to go to the station; and so they left.

'About nine o'clock the next morning, a fly from the railway station brought Miss Drummond to the house, and I told her that Sir Gilbert and Lady Linton were gone. She looked ten years older—partly because she had not taken her dressing-case with her the night before, partly because of her rage in finding that they had escaped her.

'I thought she was about to strike me. I never saw a woman in such a fury, except under the influence of drink. I had purposely refrained from giving her Sir G.'s message, in order to see how she would act, and what she would say, having before learnt some valuable information from her while in a similar condition :

' " You cursed eavesdropper !" she cried —" do you mean to tell me you don't know where they've gone ?"

' Then, finding that I was not to be frightened, she said slyly :

' " Come, Pierce, you know the secret of this house as well as I do ; I must have let it out the other night "—she alluded to a night when she had been taken with a fit of delirium in her room, and Sir G. had called me to watch her—"and, if I hadn't, you're clever enough to guess it. Come now—you know how important it is that I should not lose all I have won—tell me where they are, and I'll pay you what you like to ask."

'I replied that perhaps Sir Gilbert would give her the information she required when he came home at mid-day. This set her reflecting.

'" But if he doesn't," I added, "I may be able to let you know, as I am to follow Lady Linton."

'" You shall have a hundred pounds—two hundred—what you like, if you do !" she cried ; and then, as if mad with joy to recover the scent of her prey, so to speak, she caught me in her arms and kissed me.

'This was not all—she took me to her room, made me take some liqueur, gave me a valuable present, and then, after locking the door, professed to tell me the whole mystery, and, indeed, told me so much that, if I had any doubt as to her identity— which I had not—it would have been at once settled. But the fact is, I knew more than she chose to tell me then, having gathered the facts from her lips on two occasions, when she was in the condition I have alluded to.

'You will be surprised, madam, to find that with this knowledge I have not brought the affair to an end; but you will, on reflection, see that the woman's state- ment in itself would be insufficient to obtain a conviction, and it is that which we intend to get.

'Soon after twelve o'clock, Sir G. arrived,

and an interview between him and S. K. took place at once in the library, which I took care to overhear. S. K. began by being very violent.

'It seems that the night before she had been attacked at Melun by her usual disorder, or pretended to be so attacked, and that Sir G., instead of staying with her, as she intended he should, paid a medical man to keep her under restraint until the attack subsided. She reproached him with barbarity and many other faults, to all which Sir G. listened silently. When she was exhausted he spoke.

'"Do you want money?" he asked.

'"I want more than that, and I'll have it," she replied.

'"I don't intend that you shall," he said. "You have to pack up your things and leave this house in an hour's time.

After two o'clock the horses will be taken from the stable, and the servants will be discharged, and the house will be shut up. I am going away."

' " Where are you going ?" she asked.

' " As I don't intend to take you with me, and wish never to see you again, I shall not tell you."

' " We shall see about that," said she. " I will follow you wherever you go, if you force me to hang to the springs of your carriage."

' She was out of her senses with passion. At Sir Gilbert's direction, I packed her boxes—she would not leave his side for a moment—and they were carried to the railway station. With that woman at his elbow he paid the servants—making a liberal present to each in consideration of the abrupt termination of their service, and gave directions as to the disposal of the horses and the stock upon the ground, which he entrusted to a notary he had brought with him. Then he wrote a few words on a piece of paper, which he enclosed in an envelope, and, giving it to me, said:

' " There is a fly outside that will take you to the railway station; when you are there you will go to the address contained in this envelope."

' S. K., hearing this, made a snatch at the envelope; but I had no intention of letting her interfere with my plans, and she did not get it. She was absolutely beside herself, stupid with rage. I went away in the fly as Sir G. began to lock the doors. Outside the drive-entrance the groom was waiting, with Sir G.'s horse, saddled. If S. K. had known how Sir G. intended to leave Valvins, she surely would not have let me go away alone in the fly.

'The address on the envelope was the "Grand Hôtel du Louvre, Paris." When I registered my own box, I saw S. K.'s standing behind the barrier waiting for her. I went on to Paris by the express, and from the Place de Bastille took a fly to the Grand Hôtel. There I found Lady L., looking pale and anxious, but with a lustre in her eyes and a vivacity in her voice which showed me that her husband had not left her in doubt as to his intentions.

'"We are going to England to-morrow, Pierce," she said cheerfully.

'I asked her, as if it were perfectly immaterial to me, at what time I should have a carriage to take us to the station; and found that we were to go by

the morning express to Folkestone, by
Boulogne.

'I had taken the precaution in the
morning to tell S. K. that, in case of our
being separated, she was to go to the Hôtel
de Gibraltar, Rue St. Hyacinthe, for letters,
and my only fear was lest in her passion
she should forget this address. When
Lady L. had gone to bed—she retired
quite early, saying she was fatigued and
wished to be strong for the coming journey
—I wrote a letter to S. K., telling her to
wait in Paris until she heard from me,
and, putting it into my pocket, went to
the Hôtel de Gibraltar. Finding that
S. K. had not arrived, I left the letter
with M. Avenet, the proprietor, giving
him to understand that a grande dame
would in all probability call for it, and
that her stay in his hotel would depend

upon her receiving it. His manner convinced me that he would not neglect my instructions. However, being still anxious, I went again to the hotel the next morning (yesterday) before seven o'clock, and learnt from the garçon who was waxing the stairs that the grande dame had arrived late the night before, and now occupied the front rooms on the first floor. This was all I wanted to be sure of.

'In due time Lady Linton left Paris, taking me with her, and we arrived without accident in Folkestone, where we are now staying. Since our arrival Lady L. has received a telegram from her husband. She told me soon afterwards that Sir Gilbert would arrive to-day, and referred more than once later on to this fact, as if she feared that I suspected him of deserting her. He is to arrive this evening, and I take this opportunity of writing, as my time will in all likelihood be too closely occupied to allow of lengthy communication.

'The time for action is now close at hand. We have our hands upon John Barton ; but, as he at the last moment may refuse to give evidence against his old master, we shall not rely upon him. We have no intention of leaving open the smallest loophole of escape. We are in communication with the police authorities, and at the proper moment we shall call upon you to identify S. K., that the other accomplice may be handed over to justice. S. K. will almost certainly deny her identity, and, as it will be well to have your evidence supported by that of another who knew her formerly, I suggest that, under a plausible pretext, you shall get your husband, Mr. Gower, to accompany you—an arrangement which I think, considering all things, will not be disagreeable to you. As we may require this evidence in the course of a few days, we beg you, madam, to be in readiness to come here, or where else that circumstances require, upon receipt of telegram from me or my partner.

' Your obedient and respectful servant,

' E. PIERCE.'

CHAPTER XIII.

MESSRS. PIERCE AND PIERCE MAKE THEIR LAST MOVE.

IT was late when Sir Gilbert Linton arrived at Folkestone.

'Did you think I was never coming?' he asked, when they were alone, drawing his wife towards him.

'Do I look as if any such thought had been in my mind to-day?' she asked in reply, placing her hands on his shoulders and showing him her bright smiling face.

'No, Gertie,' he said, with a tender

sympathy in his voice. ' No. Your eyes
are bright and big, and there's not the stain
of a tear on your cheek ; yet one can see
that you have suffered.'

' Do I look older, dear ?' she asked, turning anxiously towards the glass.

' There's womanhood in your face.'

' I don't mind that. Childishness has
made me such a trouble to you, such a
trouble to myself. Oh, if I had only been
reasonable instead of giving way to an
absurd jealousy ! If you had only had a
wife who could see through appearances,
and judge every action in a calm philo-
sophical way, a wife like—like George
Eliot !'

' Why, then I shouldn't have had a wife
like you ; and that's the only sort of wife
such a man as I can love.'

' Ah !' she cried—it was half a sigh, half

a moan of delight, and her hands, slipping from his shoulders, slid round his neck, and she lay against his heart.

'I don't think I shall ever again be jealous,' she whispered presently.

'Not even of George Eliot?' he asked.

She shook her head without speaking, and pressed her smiling face closer to his breast. 'Oh no,' she thought. 'Now I am a woman, and have learnt how childish it is to be jealous, nothing can come between my husband and me to mar our happiness.'

After dinner they went out upon the balcony, which looked over the sea. It was too late to see the sea, but it was pleasant to hear it breaking on the beach and to feel the cool breeze, and have nothing to disturb the harmony of their thoughts.

Gilbert leant upon the iron railing of the balcony and smoked his pipe in tranquil silence. Gertie, with one hand slipped under his arm, stood beside him, too happy to talk.

If he had thrown away his pipe and put his arm about her, she would have been enchanted ; but as he did nothing of the kind, but kept his arms akimbo on the rail, and smoked as if he had nothing else in the world to do, she just thought that he was the finest and manliest being in existence.

Men would be no grander than women if all their thought was of love, thought she ; there is a dignity in the silence of a man which no woman ever attains to. She wondered what profound thoughts dwelt in her husband's mind, what noble reflections resulted from his silent observation.

'Ah, that fellow is going to light the gas at last!' Gilbert remarked, taking the pipe from his lips.

And sure enough the man lit the gas, and the prophecy was fulfilled.

An enormous glass globe representing the earth is the appropriate ensign of the Cosmopolitan Hotel; at night-time it is illuminated from within. When the man had lit the gas, Gilbert and his wife looked down upon the North Pole and a fair stretch of Europe.

'Can you make out Valvins, Gertie?' asked Gilbert.

'I can see where Cherbourg is, and St. Malo.'

Now in his turn Gilbert speculated upon the thoughts in his wife's mind, for she was silent after that. He did not speak for a couple of minutes ; then he said :

'And you were wondering where we should have to fly to next ?'

She did not reply ; he had rightly divined her thought ; but it seemed to her that it was a selfish speculation which ought not to have crossed her mind.

'Where should you like to go?' he asked.

She drew a little nearer to him, and, pressing his arm, said :

'Anywhere, dear, so that we may be alone.'

'There's Greenland, and there's Siberia, and there's Alaska,' he said slowly, looking down at the globe; 'but, odd as it may sound, I should say the safest place for us is that little spot marked in big letters— London.'

'Do you think so, dear?' she asked hopefully.

'I do. I don't think the fiend would come to us there, not at any rate in the shape we most detest.'

'I think London is a very nice place, then.'

'So is Folkestone just now, and I'm inclined to think it's safe also. We might stay here—not in this confounded hostelry —until October, say, and then go to town for the winter—eh?'

Gertie made a little mental calculation, and declared that October would do very well for her; and then her thoughts ran off in speculations, and she felt how pleasant it would be to have dear old Mrs. Simpson with her when—when the time came.

'Then so it shall be,' said Gilbert, knocking the ashes from his pipe and rising from the railing. 'And to-morrow, while you are busy with your needle, I'll unearth a house-agent and see if I can find a decent habitation not too near the brass band. Now give me a kiss, love, and go to bed.'

While Pierce was arranging Gertie's hair for the night she said:

'If it is not inconvenient to madam, I should like half a day's holiday before madam leaves Folkestone. I have friends living at Deal.'

'Certainly, Pierce. You shall have two or three days if you like. I shall be most happy to mark my sense of your attention and fidelity. You can go to-morrow, if that will suit you.'

'A week's time will suit me just as well, if madam intends staying at this hotel so long.'

'I don't know how long we shall stay at this hotel; probably we shall stay here only a few days; but that makes no difference to me.'

It made, however, a good deal of difference to Mrs. Pierce. She reflected for a short time, and then, in her quiet precise manner, said that, with madam's permission, she would see her friends the next day.

'Go the very first thing, Pierce,' said little Lady Linton. 'I can do very well with the service of the hotel, and you need not return until you find that your holiday has been long enough.'

When Pierce had done all that was to be

done, and left her mistress, she put on her bonnet, slipped out of the hotel by the servants' passage, and went to the telegraph-office.

She wrote out two telegrams ; one :

' From	' To
' E. PIERCE,	' MISS DRUMMOND,
'Folkestone.	' Hôtel de Gibraltar,
	' Rue St. Hyacinthe,
	' St. Honoré, Paris.

'Sir	Gilbert	and	Lady	Linton
leave	here	to-morrow	night	without
me	I	shall	be	on
the	landing	steps	Folkestone	at
five	in	the	afternoon	to
meet	the	passengers	arriving	by
the	express	from	Paris'	

The other :

'From	'To
'E. Pierce,	'Mrs. G. Gower,
'Folkestone.	'Gauntly House,
	'Camden Square,
	'London.

'S.	K.	will	be	here
to-morrow	afternoon	please	be	here
with	Mr.	G.	to	confront
her	I	shall	be	on
the	platform	of	the	Folkestone
station	to	meet	the	express
leaving	London	L.	C.	D.
Victoria	ten	forty	five	a. m.
you	will	recognise	me	standing
by	the	main	exit	dressed
in	plain	black	costume	with
one	glove	in	my	left
hand	and	a	small	leather
bag	in	my	right	I
shall	assume	to	have	been
in	your	service	previous	to
second	marriage'			

When she had delivered the papers and paid the fees, she returned to the Cosmopolitan ; but the next morning she repeated the messages for fear of accidents. Then she went to arrange matters with her husband and the officers from Scotland Yard.

CHAPTER XIV.

THE morning was so charming that Gilbert, instead of searching for a house, took his wife out in a boat. They came back to the hotel and had lunch at two; then, the afternoon being sultry, he was easily persuaded to forego the expedition he had planned and pass the time in Gertie's company. But about five o'clock a breeze sprang up, and he determined to find a house-agent.

'If there is anything in the neighbourhood, I may perhaps go to look at it; if, on the other hand, it's a case of going far from home, I shall put the business off till to-morrow,' he said. 'At any rate, I shall be home in time for dinner—seven or half-past, say;' and with that he went away.

As soon as his back was turned, Gertie fetched from its hiding-place in the adjoining bedroom that precious parcel of needle-work she had brought with her from Valvins.

Pierce had gone out early in the morning, and she was alone. They knew no one at Folkestone, so she felt absolutely secure for three or four hours of delightful work.

She was so happy that she could have sung over her work had she not had so much to think about. She didn't wish to think of the dreadful time bygone; nevertheless, as she smoothed the little robes out and looked at them, she could not but remember the awful night when she had gathered them up in the dark under her mantle and carried them pressed against her aching heart.

It was a pleasant transition from that hour of agony to recollect what happened when she and her husband were in the train together, and he proved to her how unwise her jealousy was, and showed her the real letter he had received from Miss Drummond, and promised her that she should suffer no more, and that in a few days he would join her in England to live like the hero and heroine of a fairy-tale—happy ever after.

And in making this concession to her he had sacrificed none of his own manly dignity. He had not revealed the secret which he considered unfit for her to know; that would have been unbecoming to him as a man, and unkind to her, for her shame would have been multiplied tenfold by a

confession wrung from him by her folly. He
had kept his word—as he always did—and
now they were united again, and nothing.——

At that moment she heard the door of
the bedroom open. No one surely would
come in without knocking; nevertheless
she pushed her chair back, in order to get
a view of the inner room.

With a cry of terror she dropped the
work from her hands and clutched at the
arms of the chair in which she sat.

In the doorway of the bedroom stood
Miss Drummond.

Was it really she, or merely some de-
lusive vision resulting from the mental excitement she had lately undergone? Miss
Drummond spoke, and settled the question.

'Are you alone?' she asked, not in her
customary tone of languid indifference, but
shortly and sharply.

'How dare you come here? What right

have you here?' Gertie asked, rising, the knowledge that this woman was her husband's enemy giving her a force which she had hitherto lacked.

'What right have I here?' echoed Miss Drummond. 'Why, rather more than you! Where's Gilbert?'

She stepped into the room and cast a rapid glance round, as if seeking for some trace of him.

Gertie noticed a great change in her appearance. She looked ill and old ; her eyes were bloodshot, the sacs under the lower lids distended; her face was puffy, and had a grey unwholesome tint; the heavy cheeks seemed to hang loose from the cheek-bones; her hair was disordered, and her dress was creased and crumpled with the voyage. She had come straight from the boat, and given not one thought to her looks.

'Where's Gilbert?' she repeated, turning about to fix her eyes upon Gertie.

'He is not here; and I request you to leave my room,' said Gertie.

'He was here an hour ago. I shall wait until he returns.' She seated herself as she spoke.

'You will do no such thing,' said Gertie, going across the room towards the bell.

'Stop!' cried Miss Drummond, rising quietly from her chair, and putting her hand in the pocket of her mantle. 'If you touch that bell, I will fire.'

Gertie turned in quick alarm, and found that Miss Drummond held in her hand that small silver-mounted revolver which had been her constant terror at Valvins, where it lay always upon the little table in the visitor's chamber.

'What are you going to do?' she asked.

'Nothing, if you are reasonable,' replied Miss Drummond. 'If you are not, I shall shoot you—or some one else. Don't be a fool, and no harm shall come to you. Sit down ; I have something to tell you.'

Gertie hesitated a moment ; then, with a woman's dread of violence, she sank in the chair by which she stood.

Miss Drummond drew a chair to the table, and sat down before it, resting her arms upon it and still holding the revolver.

'I am not afraid to use a pistol,' she said, 'and I'll tell you why—I am a murderess !'

Gertie shrank back in her chair, her heart contracting with horror.

'You know what happened at Monkden?' the woman continued. 'Well, I am guilty of that murder.'

When she was most tortured with jealous suspicion, it had occurred to Gertie that possibly this woman was Sophia Kirby; but she had banished the thought from her mind as being too horrible, too wildly unjust. To accuse even in imagination her husband of harbouring the wretch who had killed his wife was infamous!

'I murdered that woman because she was loved by John Barton—a man who fascinated me, and, if I had loved Gilbert half as well, I should have murdered you before now. I am mad at times—I suppose you know that—Gilbert has told you, I dare say; if he hadn't, you might guess it by my being here now—where I might have been recognised and apprehended by the first man I met on landing. A word from you would do it. But I am inclined to think that you will render me another kind of justice when you know all I have come to tell you.'

The perspiration was standing in beads upon her livid face. She laid down the revolver and threw off her mantle; then she flung her bonnet aside, and loosened her collar.

'I told you that I am mad sometimes,' she said, leaning forward with her arms on the table again, and taking the revolver into her hand. 'When I drink too much I am mad, when I'm jealous I'm mad. Sometimes I'm drunk and jealous at the same time; then I'm dangerous. I've been in that condition for two or three days now—ever since Gilbert shook me off from him at Valvins and galloped off, leaving me a raving maniac in the road. I tried to shoot him, and, if I had not been in such a frenzy of rage, I should have hit him. You think

he did well to leave me there; you look
upon him as a god, and think that he can
do no wrong. I have come to undeceive
you. He had no right to turn me out of
that house, to shake me off as if I were
vermin, to leave me there in the road un-
covered, mad, with a pistol in my hand.
It must have occurred to him that in my
desperation I might kill myself; yet, when
he heard that shot, he did not turn his head
to find at whose heart it had been aimed.
He must have said to himself—" I have had
enough of her ; she is good for nothing. If
she takes away her own worthless life, so
much the better." Perhaps ninety-nine
men in a hundred would acquit him ; but
you cannot. That was not a god who did
that—not even a good man.'

'You had no claim to his protection,'
said Gertie shortly.

' No claim !' cried the woman furiously ; and she struck the table with the butt of the revolver.

' No,' Gertie answered, undaunted.

Miss Drummond threw herself back in her chair and crossed her arms. The barrel of the pistol pointed at Gertie, and she saw it without flinching, now that she, had to defend her husband.

After some moments, in which Miss Drummond never took her eyes from Gertie's face, and seemed to be considering how she could make the justice of her cause visible to one so blinded with love, she spoke :

' I shall make you comprehend that I have a claim to his protection, or I shall have come here for nothing. I don't expect anything from Gilbert's sense of justice now, but I do from yours. And I have a claim to your consideration and your sympathy as well. When I was at Valvins, I had the right to say to you, "Go out of this house ; it is mine. You have no right to be here !" '

There was a ray of suspicion in Gertie's look which Miss Drummond saw.

' No,' she said, ' I am not mad ; what I say is quite apart from the subject of my mania. I tell you that with a couple of words I could have turned you out of that house and separated you for ever from Gilbert ; but I knew what I might expect from him by taking such a measure, and I thought to effect the same thing with more advantage to myself. I tried to get you out of the way and keep Gilbert to myself. I failed, being flung aside myself, and losing Gilbert as well. Now I have no alternative but to separate you from him——'

'Nothing shall separate us,' cried Gertie; 'if he shares your guilt—if he——'

'Oh, he had no hand in the murder, as you will see in a moment! That's not it— the reason why you must give him up to me—why you must go from this room, and never see him again——

She shifted her chair to come nearer to Gertie, and, putting one hand on her knee, and letting the other with the pistol fall by her side, she leant forward to speak, with a wicked gleam of pleasure in her eyes. There was a knock at the door at that very moment.

Gertie sprang to her feet, as if some one had come to deliver her from a terrible fate. Perhaps it was Gilbert himself!

'Wait; you shall hear!' cried the woman, clutching at Gertie's arm.

The door opened, and the servant who had knocked entered; but she was not to be stopped ; and leaning still closer, she whispered hoarsely :

'I am his wife !'

Gertie fell back into her seat as if she had been stunned.

CHAPTER XV.

THE END OF MRS. GOWER'S LABOURS.

THE servant who entered the room was Pierce. Gertie, overwhelmed by the discovery which had just been made to her, could see nothing singular in the fact that she had returned from Deal before her time.

Pierce presented a card. Gertie looked at it apathetically for several minutes, unable to detach her thoughts from the words that seemed perpetually to echo in her mind.

'The lady wishes to see madam upon a matter of importance,' said Pierce.

Gertie shook her head, as if to disembarrass herself of the cloud that enveloped her faculties. Then, having read the card once more, she started to her feet—looking from it to Miss Drummond in horror. Her ear caught the sound of a voice outside. Pierce, going to the door quietly, put her foot against the bottom of it and her hand upon the lock.

' Look, look!' whispered Gertie, putting the card in ' Miss Drummond's ' hand.

'Miss Drummond' shrugged her shoulders.

' What does it matter?' she asked.

' Think, think !' cried Gertie. ' Oh, hide yourself ! She is coming! For God's sake go into that room !'

Some one pushed the door from without. Pierce's toe acted as a wedge.

'She is here, she is here!' Gertie ejaculated, dropping her voice.

The woman looked at her with a kind of pitying interest, and then, with another shrug of her shoulders—as if the thing was scarcely worth discussion—she went slowly from the room into the adjoining chamber and closed the door.

Pierce withdrew her foot, and the door opened. Mrs. Gower entered with a quick impatient step, and, stopping abruptly, looked round the room and then at Pierce, who silently withdrew.

'Where is she?' asked Mrs. Gower, in a tone of suppressed fury, finding no one in the room but Gertie. 'Where is that woman?'

'This is my room. I do not understand what you want!'

'I want that woman—Sophia Kirby!'

'She is not here.'

'She is here! She came into this room half an hour ago!'

'I give you my word of honour, Sophia Kirby is not here,' Gertie cried, with all the firmness she could muster.

'Your word of honour! What value do you think I attach to that? If you have connived at her escape, you shall suffer for it. You and that wretch—your husband—together!'

'She has not been here, and I have not connived at her escape. And if you speak——' She faltered and stopped.

'Oh, I know you better than you imagine! Ah, will you tell me now that Sophia Kirby is not here?' saying this, Mrs. Gower picked up from the shadow of the table the bonnet the woman had cast aside. 'She is here!' she continued, raising her voice and stamping her foot. 'And you have concealed her, that your husband's complicity with her in the murder of my daughter may not be discovered. But she will not escape. The police are in the house, and every exit is guarded.'

Gertie put her hand upon the table for support, and looked at Mrs. Gower in silent terror.

'You have reason to fear!' cried Mrs. Gower exultingly. 'Your day of triumph is over, and mine begins. Every action and thought of your life from the time you first met Gilbert Linton is known to me. I know how you have held me up to ridicule, conspired with my fool of a husband and my children to deceive and mock me. I know how you made love to Gilbert Linton in my daughter's lifetime, how you

led him to the act which made him free to
marry you. I set the detectives on your
track, suspecting your husband's guilt.
Your woman Pierce was in my pay, and
reported all that happened to me. We
advertised for Sophia Kirby, and gave her
your address. We helped her to excite
your jealousy; we set her again upon your
track when you came here, and we procured
the warrant and officers for her arrest.
And do you think at the last moment we
are to be thwarted by you?'

'You have no proof that the woman
you have tracked to this room is Sophia
Kirby.'

'No; but we will have. I know her.
I will unmask the creature who calls herself Miss Drummond. She is in that
room.'

She made a rapid movement towards the

door. Quicker than she, Gertie ran to the
door, standing before it, facing Mrs.
Gower.

'You must not pass—you shall not go
in that room!' she panted. 'Oh, for the
love of Heaven, go and send the officers
away, if it is true that you have brought
them here!'

'True! You shall see!' She turned
about to go to the opposite door; but Gertie
flew to her side and held her arm.

'For mercy's sake,' she cried—'for
mercy's sake, do nothing rashly! It is for
your own happiness I speak. Listen to
me.'

'I will not listen to you! I will have
no mercy. I will not rest until your
husband and that woman are brought to
justice!'

She struggled to get to the door, Gertie

still clinging to her arm and imploring her in broken sentences to desist. She had her hand upon the lock when Gertie gasped:

' Listen, listen! It is not Sophia Kirby, I swear—Sophia Kirby is dead! It was she who was murdered—she, not your daughter. Pierce has misled you.'

' What!' exclaimed Mrs. Gower. ' What Sophia Kirby dead! Who murdered her ?'

A bolt was shot in the lock of the bed-room door, a handle turned ; the door opened, and there stood the woman Mrs. Gower had hunted down.

' O God!' she shrieked, flinging up her hands; as if to shut out that object from her view ; and then, falling back against the door, she muttered, ' My daughter!'

CHAPTER XVI.

TIBI SERIS, TIBI METIS.

GILBERT had looked at two houses; the agent had yet another to show, situated at the other side of Folkestone. Gilbert looked at his watch—

'Just six—time enough for a dip in the sea before dinner, and that's all,' he reflected.

Promising the agent to meet him the next morning and renew the search, he turned on his heel and strolled away towards the beach.

Presently he found that a gentleman and four young ladies were in front of him. They occupied the whole of the path ; they sauntered a little slower than he ; to pass them he must step into the road — that is how he came to notice them.

A gentleman with four daughters is not an uncommon sight in Folkestone, even though the gentleman be stout and short and clad with scrupulous respectability in black cloth, and his daughters be voluble ; but this gentleman in front was so excessively respectable and the young ladies so very voluble, that Gilbert could not for two minutes doubt that it was Mr. Gower and his girls.

Then one of the girls looked across the

road—as young ladies do when they hear
a gentleman's footstep in the rear, and
catching a glimpse of Gilbert with the
corner of her eye, turned rapidly to her
sisters and seemed to be communicating
a suspicion ; after which they all turned
their heads furtively, Mr. Gower included.
to look on the other side of the road.
Gilbert saw the profiles of the whole
family, and the next moment they were
upon him.

'Oh. who ever would have thought to
meet you here?' 'Have you brought
little Lady Linton with you?' 'Where
are you staying?' 'When did you come?'
'How is she?' These were the questions
which Gilbert singled out from the many
and replied to.

'I don't know who expected to meet me
here; and I have brought Gertie; and she

is very well ; and we came quite recently ;
and, if you want to know where we are
staying, you had better come with me.
The house is large enough to hold you
all, and I have no doubt the cook will
be equal to the occasion. What's the
matter, Gower ?'

Mr. Gower alone had held his tongue,
and, with his feet planted apart, was
poking a hole in the path with the end
of his umbrella, in a fit of gloomy abstrac-
tion.

'Oh, pa's been catching it!'

'And he won't tell us a word about it,
a disagreeable old thing! Ma's here, you
know.'

'We were all brought here this morning,
and we didn't know a word about it last
night.'

'There's a mystery!'

'Ma's been going about the house with a three-act-drama look in her face for months.'

'She's gone somewhere now, and pa won't tell us where.'

'Pa can keep his secret; he'll want us to keep one before long, perhaps.'

'Pa's like that gentleman in the "Arabian Nights," whose wife ate nothing but boiled rice in public; he's found out that ma's a ghoul, and don't want us to know her favourite churchyard.'

'Look here!' said Mr. Gower at length. 'Never mind what I'm like. Just you go down on the beach and throw stones in the sea. You've done nothing but bother me the whole afternoon. I won't have it! You've no more respect for me than if I were a little boy. Go on in front—I want to speak to you, old man,' he added, drawing Gilbert aside. 'Where's your wife?'

'I left her at the hotel a couple of hours ago.'

'Then you go back to her as quick as you can. I won't detain you with useless explanation. All I need tell you is that my wife and that woman who was staying with you in France are there. She wanted me to go there with the girls, but——'

Gilbert waited to hear no more. Without a word, he bolted off to the hotel.

At the foot of the stairs a couple of men were stationed, who would have stopped him; he thrust them aside and ran up two steps at a time. A group of people stood in the passage. Pierce and three or four men were before the door of his room, Pierce and one of the men with their ears at the panel.

Just then he heard the crash of a body falling against the door on the inner side. Those who stood on the outer side started back. He tried the handle, and then, putting his shoulder to the door, forced it open and entered. One of the men would have followed; but the door slammed to, crushing his finger, and causing him to draw back with a howl. Mrs. Gower it was who threw her weight against the door, and, shutting it, quickly turned the key.

Gilbert stood panting for breath in the presence of the three women. Gertie sat. with her hands clasped and her head bowed down. Mrs. Gower, now that she had fastened the door, stood with her back to it, staring wildly at her daughter, who alone seemed indifferent to the peril in which she stood. She looked from Gertie to her husband, and then to her mother, and, with a contemptuous laugh, threw herself upon a couch by the bedroom door.

'This is what you have brought me to amongst you,' she said.

Gilbert went to Gertie's side.

'No, no,' she said quickly. 'You must go to her—you must save her—she is your wife!'

'This is my mother's doing,' said Lady Linton stretching her arms out on either side and resting them on the back of the couch as she fixed her venomous eyes upon Mrs. Gower. 'It seems that she gave me the clue to your hiding-place at Fontainebleau, set this trap for me, and lured me into it——'

There was a heavy knock at the door.

'Save yourself, save yourself! Don't

you hear?' Mrs. Gower cried. in a voice hoarse with terror.

' Perhaps you'll tell me how I am to save myself, or. better still, you yourself will save me with the same cunning you have employed for my destruction !'

' Is the outer door of the bedroom locked?' asked Gilbert.

' Yes ; the key is in my pocket,' said Lady Linton. ' If Mrs. Gower will have the goodness to send away the police-officers she has brought here to arrest me, we can go out that way.'

The knock was repeated, and a man's voice demanded admittance.

Gertie started from her seat and appealed to Gilbert.

' She is your wife, Gilbert ; she must be saved,' was all she could say.

Lady Linton sat unmoved on the couch,

never taking her evil eyes from her mother.

'I owe you a good deal, madam,' she said. 'I might have been a very ordinary woman without your fostering care—a draper's assistant, as you were, perhaps—no more ; but you have raised me step by step to my present position. You ought to be proud of your handiwork. Not many women are so talked about in the newspapers as I shall be.'

While she spoke a conference was going on in the passage outside. Mrs. Gower, with her body bent, her arms drawn up, and her fingers contracted, looking like some beast preparing to spring, turned first to the door, then to her daughter, and again to the door, trying to catch the sense of all the sounds that fell upon her ear.

'They are going to burst the door,' she cried suddenly.

'You'd better save me, mother,' said Lady Linton ironically. 'Come, make another effort—something to undo the work of a life!'

Mrs. Gower heard only the bursting of the door. Clasping her hands, she made a movement towards her daughter, as if to beseech her consideration, and then turned speechless away, seeing the hopelessness of an appeal to her. She extended her arms to Gilbert.

'Gilbert!' she cried, 'help me, for God's sake! I was led to believe that the murderess was Sophia Kirby. The warrant is made out for her arrest. There is yet time to effect her escape. Only get her out of this room, and I will do the rest.'

Gilbert crossed the room, and, with an imperative sign, ordered Lady Linton to rise. She shrugged her shoulders and shook her head, without moving her arms from the back of the couch or changing her position; only, as a panel burst under the pressure thrown against it on the outside, she dropped one hand in the folds of her dress.

Gilbert caught her by the arms, and, setting his foot upon the edge of the couch, dragged her up by sheer force; then, shifting his foot and throwing his arm under her, he lifted her upon his shoulder and carried her into the adjoining room. He returned, closing the door behind him, and locking it as the door upon the other side of the room flew open, and Mrs. Pierce, with the officers, entered.

Mrs. Gower threw herself before them.

'The woman you seek is not here,' she cried.

'No; but she's in the room yonder,' replied the officer. 'Come, mum, it's no use impeding an officer in the execution of his dooty. There's no help for it.' He would have pushed his way forward, but she caught hold of his arm. 'Don't be violent, mum—it's no use at all. We've got a warrant for the arrest of the party, and——'

'Your warrant is for the arrest of Sophia Kirby!' Mrs. Gower cried, in passionate haste. 'That is useless; the woman in that room is my daughter—this lady and gentleman are witnesses. You have no legal right to touch Lady Linton, my daughter. That is her husband; he will tell you she is his wife and my daughter, not Sophia Kirby. The woman there—

Pierce—has been in error—she thought my daughter was the woman for whose arrest you have a warrant.'

'Pardon me, ma'am,' said Mrs. Pierce, with a little more energy than she was wont to exhibit. 'I have known for several weeks that the person calling herself "Miss Drummond" was in reality Lady Linton ; that is, I have suspected it very strongly. My suspicions were confirmed by the evidence of John Barton, and upon that evidence I procured a warrant for the arrest of Lady Linton.'

'Right enough, mum, so far as the warrant goes, I assure you; and now, if you please, we'll just——'

He put his shoulder against the chamber door in continuation.

The door did not give way ; he drew back, in order to launch his shoulder against the panel. There was an instant of silence, and then, before the panel was struck, the sound of a pistol-shot, a cry, and, after it, another shot came from the inner room.

The officer's shoulder fell against the door ; and, the lock breaking away, it flew open.

A thin film of blue smoke hung midway between the floor and ceiling ; beneath it, on the farther side of the room, the bed could . be seen. Athwart its length lay Lady Linton, her feet scarcely touching the ground, one arm extended sidelong, the other lying by her side.

The officer ran to the bed.

' Dead, dead !' he said. ' Shot in two places. Done us, after all !'

CHAPTER XVII.

RS. GOWER was removed from the scene of her daughter's suicide—a maniac. She never recovered her reason; and, six months after the tragedy which she had brought about, she, eluding the vigilance of her keepers, put an end to her own wretched existence.

Unhappily this was not the only evil that resulted from that terrible event. Little Lady Linton's baby was prematurely born,

and died a few hours after. This was a
great grief to the young mother, but
happily it is the last to record here. It is
four years since she wept over the little
robe she had prepared for her child; but in
those years she has had no other cause to
weep. The tears may have sprung into
her gentle eyes, but they have been tears
of compassion for the woes of others, or
tears of happiness and love, or of pride.
There is an inexhaustible fountain in the
souls of all good women, from which such
tears are drawn.

There are many calls upon her compassion, for she has become the Lady Bountiful
of that part of Devonshire in which she and
her husband have settled. If any poor
soul wants help, little Lady Linton is
straightway called upon, and never has any-

one left her gates without blessing that gracious little lady.

'It's a mistake to give in that way, Gertie,' says her husband. 'One half of the people who come for relief don't deserve it.'

'And the other half?' asks Gertie, with a twinkle in her eye and a smile about her lips. 'Shall the deserving half be punished for the faults of the undeserving?'

'Your political economy is bad,' says Gilbert ; ' but your heart, little wife '—and he takes her up in his arms—' Heaven forbid any teaching of mine should change that!'

And then her children—for she has two now—demand her constant solicitude. Children must have teeth, and by a natural consequence must cry ; and is it possible that with such a nature as hers she can hear the cry of an infant untouched?

Joy in the possession of her beautiful children, and in the love of a husband which is steadfast and strong, and pride in the public recognition of his manliness and wisdom—he has been solicited to stand for the representation of his borough in Parliament at the forthcoming election— each emotion in its turn dims little Lady Linton's big eyes with a tear. And so she passes out of this history.

Dear old Mrs. Simpson has given up her shop to William, and gone to take care of Mr. Gower and keep his house in order. It became obvious, soon after the death of Mrs. Gower, that something of the kind was advisable.

Mr. Gower abused his newly recovered liberty 'like a monkey when he gets his

chain off,' some one—I fear it was one
of his daughters—said. Loo-parties and
suppers were much too frequent on Clap-
ham Common, whither Mr. Gower had
removed, and the girls had more freedom
than was proper for young ladies of such
volatile spirits. So granny went to live
with them, and brought them, by her
gentle guidance, into that happy state of
moderation which partakes neither of
license nor irksome restraint.

The year before last Mr. Headlam,
having obtained a living through Sir
Gilbert Linton's influence, married Beatrice;
and now he is publishing the banns of her
sister Edith and Mr. Langdon.

Maud received sixteen valentines last
month; but there is one that she prizes
above all the rest, not because of its particular loveliness—though it certainly is a

most exquisite affair in satin, lace, flowers and verse—but by reason of its coming from a very handsome young gentleman who lives next door, and sings, in a most lovely tenor voice, ' Come into the garden,' so loudly that it can be heard through the dividing walls.

' Go into the garden, Maud, for Heaven's sake, and let's have a little peace!' says Mr. Gower occasionally.

A word about Mr. and Mrs. Pierce, and then the pen may be laid down.

' My dear,' said Mr. Pierce to his wife, after the inquest upon Lady Linton's body, ' this is an ugly conclusion to a very ugly business; and now is a proper time for us to retire from it. This is the last private investigation that I shall ever meddle with.'

Mrs. Pierce made no reply. There was

a quiet firmness in her husband's manner which showed her the uselessness of opposition. Possibly she herself, terrified by the conclusion of her strategies, was not sorry to relinquish an occupation which entails such terrible consequences.

Mr. Pierce was never happier in landing a chub than when he pocketed the shillings given by the broker for the furniture of his private inquiry office ; and with his own willing hand he effaced from that door-post in Endell Street the name of 'Pierce and Pierce.'

After that he undertook several ventures, with no result more hurtful than the loss of a few pounds ; but at length he has succeeded in finding an occupation which seems likely to be profitable and enduring.

The reader who visited Ramsgate last year may have noticed the addition there of a new bathing establishment in every respect preferable to the rest, and in that case cannot have failed to admire the new and capacious machines, fitted up with all modern appliances, rush-bottomed chairs, 'and every luxury,' to quote from the prospectus, and provided with rose-coloured curtains and hoods that neutralize the somewhat cadaverous tint which prejudices young ladies against sea-bathing when they look in the glass on coming out of the water, and impart a hue which it gratifies even old ladies to find in their complexion. The observer also cannot have overlooked an office on the sands, with a green veranda and pots of geranium on the window-sill, and the legend, 'Reform Bathing Establishment Company,' inscribed in large letters over the door. The Reform Bathing Establishment Company is Mr. Pierce.

'It's not a dirty business,' he says, in a tone of satisfaction, and it suits him admirably.

When the wind is chill, he sits inside the office with his newspaper; when the sun shines, he sits in his chair under the veranda. You will recognise him at once—a large heavy man in slippers and loose-fitting garments, with a bandana hanging loosely out of one pocket and a stem of a pipe sticking out of another—when it is not between his lips.

Mrs. Pierce looks after the linen, keeps the attendants to their work, escorts customers into their machines, and chats with them—ferreting out more secrets from her fair customers than they would perhaps like you and me to know.

Where they raised the money for this expensive undertaking is not certain; but it is very probable that, if Sir Gilbert's nice principles prevented him from assisting Mrs. Pierce, no such scruples influenced Mr. Gower.

THE END.

BILLING AND SONS, PRINTERS, GUILDFORD.

G., C. & Co.